MISS JENN'S
HIGH SCHOOL MUSICAL SCRIPT

Design by Betty Avila

Printed in the United States of America
First Hardcover Edition, June 2020
1 3 5 7 9 10 8 6 4 2
FAC-038091-20115

Library of Congress Control Number: 2020931601

ISBN 978-1-368-06123-0

For more Disney Press fun, visit www.disneybooks.com
Visit DisneyChannel.com and DisneyPlus.com

DISNEY
HIGH SCHOOL
MUSICAL
THE MUSICAL THE SERIES

MISS JENN'S
HIGH SCHOOL MUSICAL SCRIPT

DIRECTOR'S COPY

Based on the series created by Tim Federle
High School Musical script by
Peter Barsocchini

𝐷𝒾𝓈𝓃𝑒𝓎 P R E S S
Los Angeles • New York

When I heard the high school where High School Musical
was shot had never staged a production of High School Musical,
I was shocked as an actress, inspired as a director, and triggered
as a millennial. I made it my mission as the new drama teacher
at East High to help the next generation put their mark on
this classic.

Inside my script book, you'll find:
- Audition applications and photos
- Cast List
- Musical productions
- My marked-up version of the original script
- Production notes

Can't wait for opening night!

AUDITION SCHEDULE

--Warm up with dance routine. Have
Carlos come up with something fabulous.

--Meet and greet potential cast.
Hand out audition packets with sides.

--Auditions

Have each student:

* Read sides
* Sing thirty-two bars of "Start of
  Something New"

Start auditions with Troys, then
Gabriellas, then Chads, etc.

High School Musical
Cast Audition Application
Please be sure that all writing is legible

next Armie Hammer ★

Name E.J. Caswell   Grade: Senior

What type of part are you audition for?   LEAD ___X___   CHORUS _____   ANY _____

Rehearsal Conflicts:

Please list any potential conflicts with rehearsals. More than 2 unexcused absences may result in you being removed from the production. PERFORMANCES MAY NOT BE MISSED!!!

Water Polo: Tuesdays and Thursdays after school. (I can miss if necessary. Troy takes priority.)

Performance Experience:

Please list any acting experience you have: Leads in Music Man, Fiddler on the Roof, Camelot, and homeroom acting production of Newsies!

Please list any dance experience you have: Danced in all the productions listed.

★ Classic Troy on Paper

Please list any singing experience you have: 4 yrs. voice lessons

Do you have any other talents that may be used in this production? I was made to play Troy Bolton! He is me with a basketball.

★ Lacks emotional connection to the material

High School Musical
<u>Cast Audition Application</u>
Please be sure that all writing is legible

Name _Nini Salazar-Roberts_   Grade: _Junior_

What type of part are you audition for?   LEAD _X_   CHORUS _____   ANY _____

Rehearsal Conflicts: Harmless Chorus Girl

Please list any potential conflicts with rehearsals. More than 2 unexcused absences may result in you being removed from the production. PERFORMANCES MAY NOT BE MISSED!!!

This production is my priority. I promise I will be at all rehearsals.
I'm excited to be a Wildcat!

Adorable!

Performance Experience:

Please list any acting experience you have: _Played the lead role of Marian the librarian in_
"The Music Man" at summer drama camp. Was a tree in "Brigadoon" and the back
end of a cow in "Gypsy" during my sophomore year.

Please list any dance experience you have: _I have taken ballet, jazz, and tap lessons._
But I don't consider myself a dancer.

Committed to her performance!

Please list any singing experience you have: _I have been singing since I could talk._

Do you have any other talents that may be used in this production? _I can read music. I play the piano,_
guitar, and ukulele. I spent a month at drama camp this summer working on my
skills.

stayed calm and focused when lights went out!

High School Musical
Cast Audition Application
Please be sure that all writing is legible

Name SEB MATTHEW-SMITH   Grade: JUNIOR

What type of part are you audition for?   LEAD X   CHORUS   ANY

Rehearsal Conflicts: *Auditioning for Sharpay!!! Love that. So fresh!*

Please list any potential conflicts with rehearsals. More than 2 unexcused absences may result in you being removed from the production. PERFORMANCES MAY NOT BE MISSED!!!

I HAVE CHORES ON MY FAMILY'S FARM EVERY DAY. CAN BE HERE BEFORE SCHOOL AFTER

I MILK THE COWS. IN THE EVENINGS, I JUST HAVE TO BE HOME BY DINNERTIME.

Couldn't be more wholesome!

Performance Experience:

Please list any acting experience you have: HAD ROLES IN SCHOOL PRODUCTIONS OF "GYPSY,"

"BRIGADOON." I LOVE BROADWAY SHOWS. I WAS MEANT TO PLAY THIS ROLE.

AGREE! He's perfect.

Please list any dance experience you have: I DANCED IN OUR SCHOOL PRODUCTIONS. I PRACTICE MY

STEPS IN OUR BARN.

Please list any singing experience you have: I SANG IN THE CHORUS OF OUR SCHOOL PRODUCTIONS.

I'M ALSO IN OUR CHURCH CHOIR.

Beautiful voice.

Do you have any other talents that may be used in this production? I PLAY PIANO.

High School Musical
<u>Cast Audition Application</u>
Please be sure that all writing is legible

Name _Ricky Bowen_ Grade: _Junior_

What type of part are you audition for? LEAD _X_ CHORUS _____ ANY _____

Rehearsal Conflicts: _Late to auditions!_

Please list any potential conflicts with rehearsals. More than 2 unexcused absences may result in you being removed from the production. PERFORMANCES MAY NOT BE MISSED!!!

No conflicts. I will be here.

Performance Experience:

Please list any acting experience you have: _None._ _Improvised lines. Needs work._

Please list any dance experience you have: _None._

Please list any singing experience you have: _I sing a little, mostly in the shower._
Prepared his own song and performed with guitar.
Off-the-charts chemistry with Nini. _Got a round of applause._

Do you have any other talents that may be used in this production? _I play guitar. I'm an excellent skateboarder._

☆ _Always bet on the underdog!_

High School Musical
Cast Audition Application
Please be sure that all writing is legible

Name _Gina Porter_   Grade: _Sophomore_

What type of part are you audition for? LEAD _X_ CHORUS _____ ANY _____

Rehearsal Conflicts:

Please list any potential conflicts with rehearsals. More than 2 unexcused absences may result in you being removed from the production. PERFORMANCES MAY NOT BE MISSED!!!

I just transferred to East High. I'm new to town and don't have
any potential conflicts.

New girl is super talented.

Performance Experience:

Please list any acting experience you have: _I've been acting forever. Was in the touring_
company of "Annie" when I was younger.

Already off book.

Please list any dance experience you have: _Classically trained in ballet, jazz, modern dance,_
and hip-hop.

She's amazing.

Please list any singing experience you have: _Took singing lessons when I was younger._

Can sing, too.

Do you have any other talents that may be used in this production? _I'm an experienced performer_
ready for the role of Gabriella. I can help with choreography, too.

May not be the right fit to portray innocent Gabriella

High School Musical
Cast Audition Application
Please be sure that all writing is legible

Name _Ashlyn Caswell_ **Grade:** _Junior_

What type of part are you audition for? LEAD _____ CHORUS _____ ANY _X_

Rehearsal Conflicts: _Giving off uncommon depth. PERFECT for Ms. Darbus._

Please list any potential conflicts with rehearsals. More than 2 unexcused absences may result in you being removed from the production. PERFORMANCES MAY NOT BE MISSED!!!

I'm co-captain of the robotics club, which meets during lunch hour.
I have baking club every other Thursday evening. As high
priestess of the Salt Lake Renaissance Fair, I'm booked every other
Saturday afternoon. I Will Make Rehearsals My Priority!

Performance Experience:

Please list any acting experience you have: _I have had roles in "Gypsy" and "Brigadoon."_
My cousin, EJ, and I have been putting on neighborhood plays
since we were little.

Please list any dance experience you have: _Danced in chorus, but not lead_
dance numbers.

Please list any singing experience you have: _I have been singing my whole life._
Her voice is a "WOW!"

Do you have any other talents that may be used in this production? _I play piano._

Writes songs, too.
Need Act Two power ballad!

High School Musical
Production Crew Application
Please be sure that all writing is legible

Name __Carlos Rodriguez__   Grade: __Sophomore__

What type of part are you audition for?   CHOREOGRAPHY __✗__   WARDROBE _____

                                           MAKEUP _____   SETS _____

Rehearsal Conflicts:

Please list any potential conflicts with rehearsals. More than 2 unexcused absences may result in you being removed from the production. PERFORMANCES MAY NOT BE MISSED!!!

No conflicts. I'm totally available to you at all times.

Stage Production Experience:

Please list any production experience you have: I'm the captain of the school color guard team. I know "The Big Book of Broadway" inside out.

Do you have any special talents that may be used in this production? I've seen the original High School musical thirty-seven times. I'm also very social media savvy, so I'm planning to start a Twitter campaign for our fall production.

FABULOUS!

GREAT Style!

High School Musical
Production Crew Application
Please be sure that all writing is legible

Name *Kourtney Greene*   Grade: *Junior*

What type of part are you audition for?   CHOREOGRAPHY _____   WARDROBE *X*_____

MAKEUP *X*_____   SETS _____

Rehearsal Conflicts:

Please list any potential conflicts with rehearsals. More than 2 unexcused absences may result in you being removed from the production. PERFORMANCES MAY NOT BE MISSED!!!

I have no conflicts.

Makeup is totally on point! Must get tips!

Stage Production Experience:

Please list any production experience you have: *I have been on the costume and makeup crew of such school productions as "Brigadoon" and "Gypsy."*

I also give makeup tips on my website.

Do you have any special talents that may be used in this production? *This year, I'm all about dismantling the patriarchy, and looking fabulous while also fighting for intersectional feminism. I consider it my job to make everyone in the cast look fabulous, too. I think "High School Musical" is like a period piece, and makeup and costumes should reflect that.*

LOVE, love, love!

Late add to production crew.
Ricky's BF

High School Musical
Production Crew Application
Please be sure that all writing is legible

Name __Big Red__   Grade: __Junior__

What type of part are you audition for?   CHOREOGRAPHY _____   WARDROBE _____

MAKEUP _____   SETS __X__

Rehearsal Conflicts:

Please list any potential conflicts with rehearsals. More than 2 unexcused absences may result in you being removed from the production. PERFORMANCES MAY NOT BE MISSED!!!

I have a monthly appointment with my allergist.

Stage Production Experience:

Please list any production experience you have: ___None.___

Do you have any special talents that may be used in this production? ___I'm pretty handy.___
I know how to papier-mâché. I'm an excellent skateboarder.
I can do whatever is needed. I'm here to support my boy Ricky.

Trusting my instincts on this one.
seems like an old soul.

CAST LIST

Troy Bolton.................................. Ricky Bowen
    Troy Understudy........... E.J. Caswell

Gabriella Montez...................... Nini Salazar-Roberts
    Gabriella Understudy...... Gina Porter

Chad Danforth.............................. E.J. Caswell

Sharpay Evans............................ Seb Matthew-Smith

Taylor Mckessie........................... Gina Porter

Ms. Darbus .... Ashlyn Caswell

COSTUMES

Classic Inspiration

Opening Night Looks

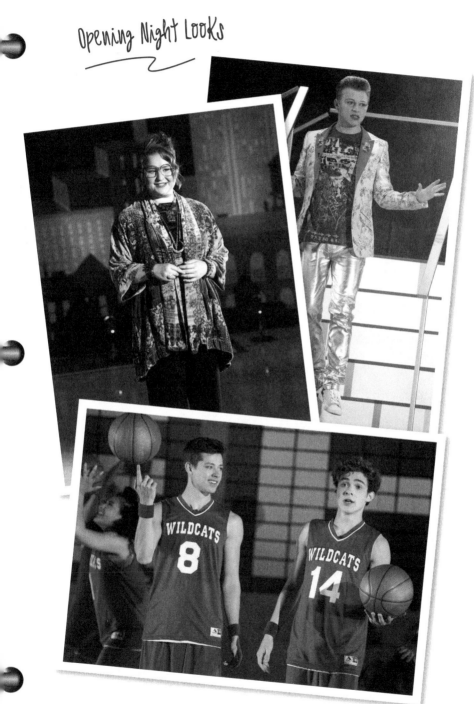

MUSICAL PRODUCTIONS

Act 1

1.) "START OF SOMETHING NEW" - Troy Bolton and Gabriella Montez

2.) "GET'CHA HEAD IN THE GAME" - Troy Bolton and Basketball Team

3.) "WHAT I'VE BEEN LOOKING FOR" - Sharpay and Ryan Evans / Troy Bolton and Gabriella Montez

4.) "STICK TO THE STATUS QUO" - Full Company

Act 2

5.) "WONDERING" - Ms. Darbus

6.) "WHEN THERE WAS ME AND YOU" - Gabriella Montez

7.) "BOP TO THE TOP" - Sharpay and Ryan Evans

8.) "BREAKING FREE" - Troy Bolton and Gabriella Montez

9.) "WE'RE ALL IN THIS TOGETHER" - Full Company

HIGH SCHOOL MUSICAL
Written by
PETER BARSOCCHINI

East High
Fall Production

Based on the story by
Bill Borden & Barry Rosenbush
and Peter Barsocchini

ACT ONE

EXT. LODGE - EVENING

Evening at a resort.

Super: NEW YEAR'S EVE

Basketball court, stage right

INT. SPORTS COURT - BASKETBALL - EVENING

An indoor sports court, modifiable for basketball, paddle tennis, etc. TROY BOLTON, early teens, shoots hoops with his dad, JACK BOLTON. Troy is handsome and athletic and gifted at BASKETBALL.

> JACK BOLTON
> (bounces ball to Troy)
> Keep working left, Troy. The guy guarding you in the championship game won't expect that. You'll torch him.

> TROY
> By going left?

> JACK BOLTON
> He'll look middle, you take it downtown.

> TROY
> Like this?

Troy spins past his father and sinks a reverse layup.

(CONTINUED)

                    JACK BOLTON
        Sweet.

TROY'S MOM appears courtside. She WEARS
a PARTY DRESS.

                    MRS. BOLTON
        Boys? Hello? Did we really fly all
        this way to play more basketball.
        It's the last night of vacation.
        The party . . . ? Remember?

                    JACK BOLTON
                 (completely forgot)
        Oh, right, right. New Year's Eve.
        Do we have to wear funny hats?

                    MRS. BOLTON
        Absolutely, and we're due in half
        an hour. Troy, they have a kids'
        party downstairs in the Freestyle
        Club.

                    TROY
        Kids' party?

                    MRS. BOLTON
        Young adults. Now go, shower up.

                                    (CONTINUED)

sitting room, stage left

INT. SITTING ROOM - ANOTHER PART OF
THE LODGE - NIGHT

Comfortably curled up in an overstuffed
chair, her face BURIED IN A BOOK (titled:
"If You Only Knew Me"), is GABRIELLA
MONTEZ. Like Troy, she's in her early
teens. All the other chairs are empty.
She's alone.

The BOOK is LIFTED RIGHT OUT OF GABRI-
ELLA'S HANDS.

                    MRS. MONTEZ
          Gabby, it's New Year's Eve.
          Enough reading.

                    GABRIELLA
          But, Mom, I'm almost done and --

                    MRS. MONTEZ
          There's a teen party. I've laid
          out your best clothes. Go.

Gabriella's mom is already dressed for
the adult party.

(CONTINUED)

                    GABRIELLA
                     (beat)
              Can I have my book back?

Gabriella heads for the room. When she's
out of her mom's sight, she OPENS THE
BOOK and reads as she walks.

                                  CUT TO:

INT. FREESTYLE CLUB - NIGHT

Packed with kids having fun at a vari-
ety of activities. The main attraction
is a KARAOKE CONTEST. An MC works the
room as TWO KIDS finish their turn at
the karaoke contest.   NEED DISCO BALL!!!
                     MC
              How about that for a couple of
              snowboarders!

ON TROY AND GABRIELLA

GABRIELLA has changed into a cute pair
of dress jeans and a sweater. And TROY
cleans up nicely, too. They wander sepa-
rately in the party, but neither of them
is having a particularly good time.
                                  (CONTINUED)

                    MC (CONT'D)
All right, let's see who is going
to rock the house next.

Lighting cue as TWO SPOTS swirl over
the crowd, and a MUSIC CUE stops the
spots.

One on TROY.

The other on GABRIELLA.

Both shake their heads, but the MC
JUMPS INTO THE CROWD and pulls them up
to the karaoke machine.

                    MC (CONT'D)
          (dragging them on stage)
          Hey, someday you'll thank me for
          this! Or not!

Troy and Gabriella are both mortified,
but they've got microphones in their
hands before they can find escape routes.
Too late now.

MUSICAL NUMBER - KARAOKE DUET - TROY,
GABRIELLA, FREESTYLE TEENS

"SOMETHING NEW," by Matthew Gerrard and
Robbie Nevil
                              (CONTINUED)

Troy starts singing . . . tentatively.
At first, he can barely get the words
of the song out.

>   TROY
>   Livin' in my own world
>   Didn't understand
>   That anything can happen
>   When you take a chance

At first, there is little interest in
the song from the partygoers.

Gabriella begins to sing in a sweet and
pure voice, just above a whisper. She,
too, is tentative and can barely get the
words out.

Troy and Gabriella have not yet made eye
contact or found any vocal confidence.
They continue to sing.

They finally look to each other for
help. And once their EYES MEET, things
change. There is an immediate chemistry
that begins to bolster them. They begin
to sing to each other, and their VOICES
gradually BLOOM. They become bolder,
louder, better.

(CONTINUED)

Suddenly, other KIDS at the party begin to
take notice. What was a scattered party is
morphing into a collective concert.

Have Carlos choreograph dancers

Looking into each other's eyes, Troy *in crowd.*
and Gabriella figuratively hold hands,
and enjoy the ride.

And as their confidence strengthens,
their singing improves. The kids at the
party are loving it. Pretty soon, it's
as if Troy and Gabriella are center
stage at the Staples Center.

The song ends. By now, the entire party
is involved. Huge applause. Troy leans
over to Gabriella.

                    TROY
          I'm Troy.

                    GABRIELLA
          Gabriella.

And both have a look of kids who have
discovered a new kind of fun.

Troy and Gabriella step forward

EXT. DECK - NIGHT *from set, indicating they are*
                     moving outside.

Troy and Gabriella buzz from the moment.

                              (CONTINUED)

                    TROY
You have an awesome voice. You're
a singer, right?

                  GABRIELLA
Just church choir is all. I tried
to do a solo and nearly fainted.

                    TROY
Why's that?

                  GABRIELLA
I took one look at all the people
staring only at me, and the next
thing I knew I was staring at the
ceiling. End of solo career.

                    TROY
The way you sang just now, that's
pretty hard to believe.

                  GABRIELLA
This is the first time I've done
something like this! It was so
cool!

                    TROY
Completely.

                  GABRIELLA
You sounded like you've done a
lot of singing, too.

                                    (CONTINUED)

                    TROY
         Oh sure, lots. My showerhead is
         very impressed with me.

    Troy and Gabriella want to hold on to
    the moment, but aren't sure how to do it.

GET FIREWORK SOUND EFFECTS!   **THEN--**

    We HEAR a COUNTDOWN to midnight coming
    from the party behind them. Then noise-
    makers, and FIREWORKS start exploding.

    Both are aware that people KISS at mid-
    night on New Year's Eve, and both are
    feeling awkward.

                  GABRIELLA
See if Vanessa   I guess I'd better go find my mom
Hudgens's phone and wish her a happy new year.
from the original is
still available on eBay.   TROY
                   Me too. I mean, not your mom. My
         mom . . . and dad. I'll call you
         tomorrow.
    (pulls out his PHONE, snaps her photo,
         then hands her the phone)
         Put your number in.
                              IS IT IN OUR SHOW BUDGET?
                  GABRIELLA
         You too--

                              (CONTINUED)

They switch phones and program numbers.

Gabriella starts to leave.

                    TROY
          Singing with you is the most fun
          I've had on this vacation.
          (he's shuffling around)
          Where do you--

AGAIN:
firework sound
effects!

Fireworks EXPLODE, drowning him out.

Gabriella is at the stairs . . . she
waves, and then she's gone.

Troy stays put . . . he knows something
really cool just happened, even if he's
not certain what it was.

                    Gabriella exits stage left.

                    FADE TO:

SUPER: ONE WEEK LATER - ALBUQUERQUE,
NEW MEXICO

(CONTINUED)

EXT. EAST HIGH SCHOOL - MORNING -
ESTABLISHING SHOT

~~DELETE SCENE~~

~~Kids arriving, buses unload, students
showing off new clothes, other kids leaning
out of bus windows (bus is STOPPED) to call
to friends, others sharing stories on the
first morning back from winter vacation.~~

INT. EAST HIGH / LOBBY - MORNING

Kids greet each other, catching up.
TROY enters courtyard. Banner reads:
Happy New Year, Wildcats. As soon as
kids spot Troy, it's high fives, low
fives, and side fives.

*Need locker backdrop
for sets.*

                    CHAD
        Yo, doggie! Troy my hoops boy!

CHAD is the curly-haired number two to
Troy's number one. Troy is surrounded
by other members of his basketball team,
including ZEKE BAYLOR and JASON CROSS.

                    TROY
        Hey, Chad. Dudes, Happy New Year.

(CONTINUED)

                         CHAD
                  (like a televangelist)
             Oh, yes, it _will_ be a Happy
             Wildcat New Year, because in two
             weeks we are going to the champi-
             onships, with _you_ leading us to
             infinity and beyond!

     NEW ANGLE

     SHARPAY and RYAN EVANS arrive, brother
     ~~and sister~~, co-presidents of the Drama
     Club. RYAN wears whatever Leonardo Di-
     Caprio wore in his last TV interview,
     and SHARPAY ~~is a Barbie-doll beauty~~
     ~~dressed to within an inch of her life,~~
     ~~plus she~~'s never met a blow dryer she
     didn't like.

Sharpay is dressed in a pink blazer
and cool metallic pants   **NEED HEDWIG EYE MAKEUP!**
                         ZEKE
                  (watching Sharpay)
             Hey, the ice princess has returned
             from the North Pole.

                         CHAD
             Yeah, she probably spent the
             holidays the way she always does.

                         TROY
             How's that?

                                              (CONTINUED)

                    CHAD
Shopping for mirrors.

CHAD HOWLS like a wolf, joined by his
teammates.

NEW ANGLE- TAYLOR MCKESSIE, president
of the Chemistry Club, arrives with a
couple of her brainiac girlfriends.
Taylor is tall and imperious and eyeballs the howling display by Chad and
his buddies.

                    TAYLOR
            (off Troy and the boys)
        Ah, behold the zoo animals her-
        alding the new year. How tribal.

The BELL RINGS.

INT. SCHOOL / HOMEROOM HALLWAY - DAY

As students empty into their homerooms,
around a corner comes the SCHOOL PRIN-
CIPAL escorting-

GABRIELLA MONTEZ and her MOTHER.

(CONTINUED)

                    PRINCIPAL MATSUI
We're consistently rated in the
top ten academically in the state,
and I think you'll also find this
a wonderful community atmosphere.

GABRIELLA'S POV - peers through a window
in the homeroom door. There is first-day-
back CHAOS inside.

                    GABRIELLA
          Mom, my stomach--

                    MRS. MONTEZ
--is always nervous on the first
day at a new school. You'll do
great. You always do, and I've
made my company promise that I
can't be transferred again until
you graduate.

                    PRINCIPAL MATSUI
              (trying to be helpful)
Worry not, Gabriella. I've reviewed
your impressive transcripts. I
expect your light will shine very
brightly here at East High.

                    GABRIELLA
              (whispers to her mom)
I don't want to be the school's
"freaky genius girl" again.

                              (CONTINUED)

                    MRS. MONTEZ
                    (hugs her)
              Just be Gabriella.

INT. SCHOOL / HOMEROOM - DAY

The homeroom teacher and THEATER ARTS
(Drama) instructor is MS. DARBUS, a
flamboyantly dressed woman with (glasses)
(almost larger than her face.)
                   Get really big glasses for Ashlyn!!!
And her HOMEROOM design, for English/
Drama classes, matches her personality,
with tragedy/comedy masks on the walls,
a coffee table instead of a desk, with
director's chairs on either side . . .
looks like she's ready to host "Inside
the Actors Studio."

Gabriella ENTERS, averting her eyes,
trying to be invisible.

ON TROY - exchanging greetings with students . . . then he catches a GLIMPSE OF
GABRIELLA. Troy does a double take . . .
so many students are moving about, it's
hard for him to see.

Gabriella slips to the back of the
room, seated in a far corner.

                                    (CONTINUED)

The FINAL BELL sounds and students settle.

Troy cranes his neck, trying to see
GABRIELLA . . . could it be the same
girl from New Year's? Is it possible?

> MS. DARBUS
> I trust you all had splendid hol-
> idays. Check the sign-up sheets
> in the lobby for new activities,
> especially our winter musical.
> There'll be single auditions for
> the supporting roles, as well
> as pairs auditions for our two
> leads--

At the mention of the musical, CHAD leads
the JOCKS in a round of dry RASPBERRIES.

> MS. DARBUS (CONT'D)
> (to Chad)
> Mr. Danforth, this is a place of
> learning, not a hockey arena.

On TROY - trying to see GABRIELLA . . .
heads are in the way. He slips his CELL
PHONE from his pocket and pulls up the
PHOTO of GABRIELLA taken that last
night on vacation.

(CONTINUED)

MS. DARBUS (CONT'D)
There is also a final sign-up for
next week's Scholastic Decathlon
competition. Chem Club president
Taylor McKessie can answer your
questions on that.

Muted RASPBERRIES from CHAD and the boys.

Angle on TAYLOR.

Ms. Darbus looks up and the boys go
instantly silent.

On TROY - He pushes the SEND button on
his phone.

On GABRIELLA -- (she has not a clue
that Troy Bolton is in this school).
Suddenly, as Ms. Darbus is still
talking, a CELL PHONE starts a WILD
MUSICAL RING.

At the first RING, RYAN AND SHARPAY
immediately pull out their cell phones.
Any call must be for them, right?

(CONTINUED)

MS. DARBUS (CONT'D)
Ah, the cell phone menace returns
to our crucible of learning!
Sharpay and Ryan, your phones
please, and I'll see you in detention.

Ms. Darbus lifts a plastic BUCKET that
is LABELED: "CELL-ITARY CONFINEMENT."
She collects their phones.

But the MUSICAL RINGING CONTINUES.
Ms. Darbus searches the room. GABRIELLA
fumbles about in her backpack. Books,
pencils, brushes, and food spill to the
floor. Total humiliation. Finally, she
digs her phone from the bottom of the
backpack and SEES TROY'S PHOTO ON ITS
DISPLAY.

Troy . . . from vacation. What? How
can this be? Bewildered, she accidentally
hits ANSWER instead of END.

ON TROY - when the call is connected
GABRIELLA'S PHOTO is staring right
back at him from his phone.

By now MS. DARBUS looms over Gabriella.

(CONTINUED)

                    MS. DARBUS (CONT'D)
          We have zero tolerance on cell
          phones during class. So we'll get
          to know each other in detention.
          Phone, please . . . and welcome
          to East High, Miss Montez.

MS. DARBUS walks with her BUCKET toward
the front. Notices TROY'S PHONE.

                    MS. DARBUS (CONT'D)
          Mr. Bolton, I see your phone is
          involved. Splendid, we'll see you
          in detention, as well.

She extends the bucket for Troy's phone.

CHAD LEAPS OUT OF HIS CHAIR.

                         CHAD
          That's not even a possibility,
          Ms. Darbus, your honor, because
          we have basketball practice, and
          Troy is--

                    MS. DARBUS
          Ah, that will be fifteen minutes for
          you, too, Mr. Danforth. Count 'em.

                                        (CONTINUED)

TAYLOR
(whispers to friend)
That could be tough for Chad,
since he probably can't count
that high.

MS. DARBUS
Taylor McKessie. Fifteen minutes.

Taylor's jaw drops. She's never had
detention in her life.

Ms. Darbus whirls around.

MS. DARBUS (CONT'D)
Shall the carnage continue? Va-
cation is over, people. Way over!
Now any more comments? Questions?

JASON, the gentle giant, raises his hand.

MS. DARBUS
Jason.

JASON
So how were your holidays,
Ms. Darbus?

The BELL RINGS and kids bolt for the door.

CHAD
Sorry, man.

(CONTINUED)

INT. SCHOOL / MAIN HALLWAY - MOMENTS
LATER

TROY WAITS until his FRIENDS DISPERSE
before he approaches GABRIELLA. They
stare at each other in disbelief.

                    GABRIELLA
          I don't--

                         TROY
                    (whispering)
          --believe it.

                    GABRIELLA
          Me . . .
                         TROY
                    (whispering)
          . . . either. But how . . .

                    GABRIELLA
          My mom's company transferred her
          here to Albuquerque. I can't be-
          lieve you live here. I looked for
          you at the lodge on New Year's Day.

                         TROY
                    (whispering)
          We had to leave first thing.

                    GABRIELLA
          Why are you whispering?

                              (CONTINUED)

                    TROY

          Oh, well, my friends know I went
          snowboarding, I didn't tell them
          about the . . . singing . . .
          thing.

                  GABRIELLA

          Too much for them to handle?

                    TROY

          It was . . . cool. But, my friends,
          that's not what I do. That was,
          like, a different person.

They reach the LOBBY, where the ACTIVITY
SIGN-UP SHEETS are posted.

                    TROY
            (pointing to audition/sign-up)
          Now that you've met Ms. Darbus,
          I bet you just can't wait to
          sign up for that.

She laughs.

                  GABRIELLA

          I won't be signing up for any-
          thing for a while. I just want
          to get to know the school. But
          if you signed up, I'd consider
          coming to the show.

                                    (CONTINUED)

                    TROY
        That's completely impossible.

                  SHARPAY (O.S.)
        What's impossible, Troy? I wouldn't
        think impossible is even in your
        vocabulary.
            (indicates Gabriella)
        So nice of you to show our new
        classmate around.

SHARPAY REALIZES THAT GABRIELLA is eye-
balling the musical sign-up sheet.

                    his
Sharpay SIGNS her NAME to the list with
a flourish. Sharpay's signature swallows
up the ENTIRE LIST.

                 SHARPAY (CONT'D)
          (butter wouldn't melt . . .)
        Oh, were you going to sign up,
        too? My brother and I have starred
        in all the school's productions
        and we really welcome newcomers.
        There are a lot of supporting
        roles in the show. I'm sure we
        could find something for you.

Gabriella takes in SHARPAY'S looming
presence.

                                    (CONTINUED)

                    GABRIELLA
          No, no. I was just looking at
          all the bulletin boards. Lots
          going on at this school. Wow.
       (Indicates Sharpay's over-the-top
                  SIGNATURE)
          Nice penmanship.

Gabriella hurries away, leaving TROY with
SHARPAY.

                    SHARPAY
          So, Troy. I missed you during
          vacation. What'd you do?

                     TROY
          Practiced basketball. Snowboarding.
          More basketball.

                    SHARPAY
          When's the big game?

                     TROY
          Two weeks.

                    SHARPAY
          You are so dedicated.
             (after thought)
          Just like me. I hope you come
          watch me in the musical. Promise?

                                    (CONTINUED)

Work with Big Red on the difference between upstage and downstage. He's not getting it just yet.

CUT TO:

INT. SCHOOL / GYM - SAME DAY

The guys in midday practice. Most of the guys are running a weave drill in b.g. Troy and Chad take turns guarding each other in a little pressure drill.

> TROY
>
> Hey, you know that school musi-
> cal thing? Is it true you get ex-
> tra credit just for auditioning?

> CHAD
>
> Who cares?

> TROY
>
> It's good to get extra credit . . .
> for college and all.

> CHAD
>
> Do you think that LeBron James
> auditioned for his school musical?

> TROY
>
> Maybe.

(CONTINUED)

                    CHAD
Troy, the music in those shows
isn't hip-hop or rock, or anything essential to culture. It's
like . . . "show music." Costumes
and makeup. Frightening.

                    TROY
I thought it might be a good
laugh. Sharpay is kind of cute, too.

                    CHAD
So is a mountain lion, but you
don't pet it.

TROY turns to the TEAM.

                    TROY
              (taking charge)
All right, let's kick it in. Run
the shuffle drill.

The team falls into place.

MUSICAL NUMBER - TROY AND THE BASKET-
BALL TEAM

"GET 'CHA HEAD IN THE GAME" - by Ray Cham

                              (CONTINUED)

As the balls begin to bounce and basketball shoes squeak across the gym
floor, these percussive sounds initiate
the rhythm of the song.

We drift into a musical place watching
Troy take his role as an inspiring team
captain, singing out the practice drills.

Finally, Troy shouts out the team mantra.

>   TROY
> *Just keep ya' head in the game*
> *Keep ya' head in the game*
> *Just keep ya' head in the game*
> *Don't be afraid to shoot the*
> *outside "J"*

As Troy sings out the drills, it is
clear his team respects him in the way
they perform on the court.

Suddenly, Troy begins to sing and loses
himself in a melodic riff. He quickly
snaps back into focus before anyone can
notice (he hopes).

Suddenly, the entire gym goes black except for a light around Troy *or* all
players freeze as Troy continues to sing.

(CONTINUED)

                    TROY
        Why am I feeling so wrong?
        My head's in the game,
        But my heart's in the song.

The lights pop back on and Troy joins
the team for a "Stomp"-like basketball
dance.

The choreography is now full-out all
boy, all basketball as Troy and team
sing to the finish. The song ends, and
a well worked-out team heads for the
locker room.

Troy lags behind, already realizing
that even THINKING about the musical is
going to be a problem.

MUST figure out how to get Troy
to levitate above the basket.   CUT TO:

INT. SCHOOL / CHEMISTRY LAB - MORNING

The second-story lab overlooks an OUT-
SIDE QUAD.

The CHEMISTRY TEACHER writes equations
on the board as chem students set up

                                    (CONTINUED)

lab stations. SHARPAY is in class with
GABRIELLA, and takes the stool next to
her. TAYLOR is in the back of the room.

> SHARPAY
> So, it seemed like you knew Troy
> Bolton?

> GABRIELLA
> Not really. I just asked him for
> directions.

GABRIELLA is DISTRACTED by the EQUATION
the TEACHER is calculating on the BOARD,
and starts checking the work on her
scratch pad.

> SHARPAY
> Troy doesn't usually interact
> with new students.

> GABRIELLA
> Why not?

GABRIELLA looks at her calculation . . .
not the same as the teacher's. She's
reluctant to say anything.

> SHARPAY
> Well, it's pretty much basket-
> ball 24/7 with him.

(CONTINUED)

                    GABRIELLA
        (looking at her pad, whispers to herself)
            Pi to the eleventh power.

                    CHEM TEACHER
            Yes, Miss Montez?

                    GABRIELLA
            Oh, I'm sorry, I was just . . .

The teacher LOOKS at Gabriella's equation.

                    CHEM TEACHER
            Pi to the eleventh power? That's
            quite impossible.

The teacher enters data into her CALCU-
LATOR.

Angle on - TAYLOR, working her calc as well.

                CHEM TEACHER (CONT'D)
                    (stunned)
            I stand corrected. And welcome
            aboard.

On TAYLOR, staring at Gabriella, im-
pressed.

                                                CUT TO:

INT. SCHOOL / MAIN HALLWAY - BULLETIN
BOARD - DAY

On TROY BOLTON as he walks past the
BULLETIN BOARD--he pauses to look again
at the MUSICAL AUDITION LIST. Obviously,
he's thinking about it.

NEW ANGLE - RYAN, Sharpay's brother,
hangs nearby with a couple of the drama
club kids, NOTICES TROY staring at the
sign-up sheet.

Finally, Troy moves on, and Ryan runs up
to see if Troy added his name to the list.
SHARPAY arrives.

                    RYAN
          Troy Bolton was looking at our
          audition list.

                    SHARPAY
          Again? You know, he was hang-
          ing around with that new girl
          and they were both looking at the
          list. There's something freaky
          about her. Where did she say she
          was from?

INT. SCHOOL / LIBRARY - DAY

(CONTINUED)

SHARPAY runs a search . . . GABRIELLA
MONTEZ, SAN DIEGO.

ON COMPUTER SCREEN - NEWSPAPER ARTICLES

*"Whiz Kid Leads School to Scholastic
Championship"*

*"Sun High Marvel Aces Statewide
Chemistry Competition"*

There is a PHOTO of Gabriella holding
awards.

Sharpay PRINTS OUT THE ARTICLES.

                    RYAN
(on seeing an article about Gabriella)
          Wow! An Einstein-ette. So why do
          you think she's interested in our
          musical?

                    SHARPAY
          I'm not sure that she is. And we
          needn't concern ourselves with am-
          ateurs. But . . . there is no harm
          in making certain that Gabriella's
          welcomed into school activities
          that are . . . well, appropriate
          for her. After all . . . she loves pi.

                              (CONTINUED)

Sharpay neatly folds the ARTICLES and smiles at ~~her~~ brother. When he sees that smile, he knows the wheels are turning.

CUT TO:

INT. SCHOOL / THEATER - STAGE- LATER

Ms. Darbus conducts detention in the theater, punishment being painting scenery, mopping the stage, binding scripts.

Sharpay gives Ryan painting instructions and stands there as he executes them. Chad tries to assemble a piece of scenery, but is messing up. Troy and Gabriella exchange awkward glances from opposite sides of the stage.

TAYLOR MCKESSIE, Scholastic Club president, enters and beelines for GABRIELLA. Taylor looks like she just won the lottery.

                    TAYLOR
          (to Gabriella, beaming)
     The answer is yes!

(CONTINUED)

                    GABRIELLA
          Huh?

                    TAYLOR
          Our Scholastic Decathlon team
          has its first competition next
          week, and there's certainly a
          chair open for you.

TAYLOR SHOWS GABRIELLA THE NEWSPAPER
ARTICLES about her.

                    GABRIELLA
                    (stunned)
          Where did those come from?

                    TAYLOR
          Didn't you slip them in my locker?

                    GABRIELLA
          Of course not.

Now Taylor is confused. So is Gabriella.

ON SHARPAY - keeps his poker face, but
has his ear trained on Taylor and Gabriella.

                    TAYLOR
          Well, we'd love to have you on
          the team. We meet almost every day
          after school. Please?

                                    (CONTINUED)

                    GABRIELLA
          I need to catch up on the cur-
          riculum here before I think about
          joining any clubs.

                    SHARPAY
                  (turns around)
          But what a perfect way to get
          caught up, meeting with the
          smartest kids in school. What a
          generous offer, Taylor.

MS. DARBUS enters from the wings.

                    MS. DARBUS
          So many new faces in detention
          today. I hope you don't make a
          habit of it, though the drama
          club could always use an extra
          hand. Now, as we work, let's
          probe the mounting evils of cell
          phones. My first thought on the
          subject is--

On CHAD, trying to hide inside a piece
of scenery.

                                   CUT TO:

                                   (CONTINUED)

INT. SCHOOL / GYM - SAME TIME

The basketball team is on court ready
for after-school practice when THE HEAD
COACH enters and blows his whistle.

The COACH happens to be JACK BOLTON,
Troy's father.

                    COACH BOLTON
          Okay, let's get rolling. Two
          weeks to the big--
                    (realizes)
          Where are Troy and Chad?

INT. SCHOOL / THEATER - STAGE - MOMENTS
LATER

The students work on stage as MS. DARBUS
wanders among them, pontificating as if
this is opening night at the Old Globe.

                    MS. DARBUS
          Perhaps the most heinous example of
          cell phone abuse is ringing in
          the theater. What temerity! For the
          theater is a temple of art, a precious
          cornucopia of creative energy . . .

Ryan and Sharpay nod in somber agreement.
CHAD snores inside a FAKE TREE. COACH
BOLTON comes flying into the theater.

                                        (CONTINUED)

                    COACH BOLTON
          Where's my team, Darbus? And
          what the heck are those two doing
          here?

                    MS. DARBUS
          It's called crime and punishment,
          Coach Bolton.
           (gestures to the stage)
          And proximity to the arts is
          cleansing for the soul.

Chad stumbles out of the FAKE TREE.

                    COACH BOLTON
                 (to Ms. Darbus)
          May we have a word?
          (points to Troy and Chad)
       You two, into the gym, right now!

Troy and Chad leap up. Gabriella watches
them go. Troy snags his cell phone from
the bucket as he flies out the door.

**INT. SCHOOL / PRINCIPAL'S OFFICE --
MOMENTS LATER**

Coach Bolton and Ms. Darbus stand in
front of Principal Matsui, arms defi-
antly folded.

                              (CONTINUED)

COACH BOLTON

If they have to paint sets for
detention, they can do it tonight,
not during my practice.

MS. DARBUS

If these were theater performers
instead of athletes, would you
seek special treatment?

COACH BOLTON

Darbus, we are days away from
our biggest game of the year.

MS. DARBUS

And we are in the midst of our
auditions for our winter musical, as well! This school is
about more than just young men
in baggy shorts flinging balls
for touchdowns!

COACH BOLTON

Baskets! They shoot baskets.

PRINCIPAL MATSUI
(heard it all before)

Listen, guys, you've been having
this argument since the day . . . let
me think . . . since the day you
both started teaching here. We are
one school, one student body, ONE
FACULTY! Can we not agree on that?

(CONTINUED)

Coach Bolton and Ms. Darbus are not about to agree on anything.

> PRINCIPAL MATSUI (CONT'D)
> (to Coach Bolton)
> How's the team looking, anyways? Troy got them whipped into shape?

INT. SCHOOL / GYM- MOMENTS LATER

> COACH BOLTON
> The West High Knights have knocked us out of the playoffs three years running. Now we're one game away from taking that champion-ship right back from them! It's time to make our stand. The team is you, and you are the team. And the team does not exist unless each and every one of you is fully focused on our goal.
> (hones in on Troy and Chad)
> Am I clear?

> TEAM
> Wildcats! Getcha head in the game!

CUT TO:

(CONTINUED)

Scroll the locker backdrop in the background to make it appear like they are walking.

EXT COURTYARD - AFTER SCHOOL

Taylor and Gabriella walk together out of detention.

                    TAYLOR
          We've never made it out of the
          first round of the Scholastic
          Decathlon. You could be our an-
          swered prayer.

                    GABRIELLA
          I'm going to focus on my studies
          this semester and help my mom get
          the new house organized. Maybe
          next year.

                    TAYLOR
          But . . .

                    GABRIELLA
          What do you know about Troy
          Bolton?

                    TAYLOR
          Troy? Hmm . . . I wouldn't consider
          myself an expert on that partic-
          ular subspecies, however, unless
          you speak cheerleader, as in--

SIX CHEERLEADERS walk in a pack near
TAYLOR AND GABRIELLA. Taylor leans over
to them.

                              (CONTINUED)

                    TAYLOR (CONT'D)
                 (in cheerleader-ese)
          Isn't Troy Bolton just the hottie
          super bomb?

The CHEERLEADERS NOD ENTHUSIASTICALLY.

                       TAYLOR
                 (back to Gabriella)
          See what I mean?

                      GABRIELLA
          I guess I don't know how to speak
          cheerleader.

                       TAYLOR
          Which is why we exist in an
          alternate universe to Troy-the-
          basketball-boy.

                      GABRIELLA
          Have you tried to get to know him?

                       TAYLOR
          Watch how it works in the cafete-
          ria tomorrow when you have lunch
          with us. Unless you'd rather sit
          with the cheerleaders and discuss
          the importance of firm nail beds.

                      GABRIELLA
          My nail beds are history.

                                    (CONTINUED)

Gabriella and Taylor COMPARE CHEWED UP
NAILS.

                    TAYLOR
        Sister!

They slap hands.

                                    CUT TO:

EXT. BOLTON HOME - BACKYARD - DUSK

Troy shoots hoops under the lights in
his backyard. His father watches.

                    COACH BOLTON
        I still don't understand this
        whole detention thing.

                    TROY
        It was my fault. Sorry, Dad.

                    COACH BOLTON
        Darbus will grab any opportunity
        to bust my chops, and yours, too.

                    TROY
        (searches for the right words)
        Dad, did you ever think about trying
        something new but were afraid of
        what your friends might think?
                                    (CONTINUED)

                    COACH BOLTON
You mean working on going left?
You're doing fine.

                      TROY
I meant--what if you try something
really new and it's a disaster
and all your friends laugh at
you?

                    COACH BOLTON
Then maybe they're not really
your friends. That was my whole
point about team today. You guys
have to look out for each other.
And you're the leader.

                      TROY
Yeah, but--

                    COACH BOLTON
There are going to be college
scouts at our game next week,
Troy. Do you know what a schol-
arship is worth these days?

                      TROY
A lot?

                    COACH BOLTON
Focus, Troy.

                                        (CONTINUED)

INT. SCHOOL / HOMEROOM - NEXT DAY

Troy enters and sneaks a sheepish PEEK
at Gabriella, and catches her doing the
same thing.

> MS. DARBUS
> I expect we learned our homeroom
> manners yesterday, people. Correct?

Everyone nods.

> MS. DARBUS (CONT'D)
> If not, we have dressing rooms
> that need painting. Now, a few
> announcements. This morning
> during free period is your chance
> for musical auditions, both sin-
> gles and pairs. I'll be in the
> theater until noon, for those of
> you bold enough to extend the
> wingspan of your creative spirit.

> CHAD
> (whispers to buddies)
> What time is she due back on the
> mothership?

Scroll the locker backdrop in the background to make it appear like they are walking.

INT. SCHOOL / CHEM HALLWAY - MOMENTS LATER

> CHAD
>
> Hey, Troy, the whole team's hitting the gym during free period. What do you want to have us run?

> TROY
>
> Can't make it. I've got to catch up on some homework.

> CHAD
>
> What? Hello, it's only the second day back, dude. I'm not even behind on homework yet, and I've been behind on homework since preschool.

> TROY
>
> Catch you later.

Troy disappears into the hallway crowd. Chad is perplexed.

> CHAD
> (to himself)
> Homework? There's no way.

CHAD FOLLOWS TROY

INT. SCHOOL /CHEM HALLWAY - DAY

DELETE SCENE

As Troy weaves through the hallway, he
suddenly ducks into a classroom. Chad
peers into the classroom, SEES TROY
talking to a couple of students. But
not students Troy usually talks to.
Strange.

Chad is distracted by someone, and when
he glances back at Troy . . . TROY IS
GONE.

INT. SCHOOL / STAIRWELL - CONTINUOUS

STAIRWELL - TROY hurrying down a
stairwell, glances over his shoulder . . .
knew he was being followed.

EXT. AUTOMOTIVE SHOP - CONTINUOUS

Troy darts across the courtyard--THEN
HE SEES HIS FATHER approaching from the
opposite direction. Troy slides into
the Auto Shop.

On COACH BOLTON - he pauses, wondering
if he just saw Troy. Guess not. He shrugs
and moves on.

(CONTINUED)

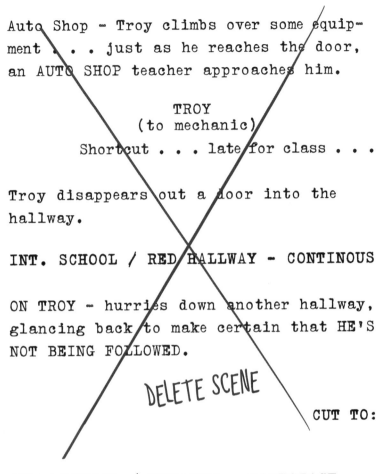

Auto Shop - Troy climbs over some equip-
ment . . . just as he reaches the door,
an AUTO SHOP teacher approaches him.

                    TROY
              (to mechanic)
          Shortcut . . . late for class . . .

Troy disappears out a door into the
hallway.

INT. SCHOOL / RED HALLWAY - CONTINOUS

ON TROY - hurries down another hallway,
glancing back to make certain that HE'S
NOT BEING FOLLOWED.

                DELETE SCENE

                              CUT TO:

INT. SCHOOL / THEATER - BACKSTAGE -
MOMENTS LATER

Troy's POV as he peers from behind cur-
tains. Kids enter the theater for the
musical auditions.

Troy grabs a mop and rolling bucket,
turns the mop upside down and uses it

                              (CONTINUED)

for cover as he rolls the bucket down a
ramp, along the side of the theater and
into the shadows in the back of the house.

Ms. Darbus, the DRAMA TEACHER, steps
forward on stage.

                    MS. DARBUS
              (going for the Tony Award)
              This is where the true expression
              of the artist is realized, where
              inner truth is revealed through
              the actor's journey, where . . .
              (snaps) Was that a cell phone?

                    KELSI
              No, ma'am. That was the warning
              bell.

KELSI is a shy little COMPOSER who
lives in fear of Ms. Darbus, and of
just about everyone else, as well.

                    MS. DARBUS
                (to the students)
              Those wishing to audition must
              understand that time is of the
              essence. We have many roles to
              cast and the final callbacks
              will be next week. First, you'll
              sing a few bars and then I will
              give you a sense of whether or

                                        (CONTINUED)

not the theater is your calling. Better to hear it from me than from your friends. Our composer, Kelsi Nielson, will accompany you and be available for rehearsals prior to callbacks. Shall we?

KELSI sits at the PIANO to play for the auditions.

Ms. Darbus takes a seat in the FRONT ROW and braces herself for the auditions.

AUDITION MONTAGE - STUDENTS

"WHAT I'VE BEEN LOOKING FOR" - by Adam Watts & Andy Dodd

Rapid-fire snippets of VARIOUS INDIVIDUAL STUDENTS singing for Ms. Darbus. On Ms. Darbus - years of student auditions have frayed her to the snapping point.

                    FIRST SINGER
                     (off-key)
          It's hard to believe that
          I couldn't see
          That you were always right
          beside me

DELETE SCENE

(CONTINUED)

MS. DARBUS
Uh-huh. Yes, thank you. Next.

Next up is ALAN, a bad singer but VERY
sharp dresser.

ALAN
It's hard to believe that I
couldn't see . . .

MS. DARBUS
Alan, I admire your pluck. As to
your voice . . . those are really
nice shoes you're wearing. Next.

CYNDRA
(high-pitched)
. . . so lonely before I finally
found what I've been looking . . .
for

CYNDRA's audition concludes with a
piercing high note.

MS. DARBUS
Ah . . . Cyndra. What courage to
pursue a note that has not been
accessed in the natural world.
Bravo! Brava! How about . . .
the spring musical.

(CONTINUED)

BACK OF THE HOUSE - Troy watches the auditions from the shadows in the back of
theater. He feels a tap on his shoulder.

It is GABRIELLA.

> GABRIELLA
> Hey! You decided to sign up for
> something?

> TROY
> No. You?

> GABRIELLA
> No.
> (beat)
> Why are you hiding behind a mop?

Troy awkwardly pushes the mop out of
the way.

> GABRIELLA (CONT'D)
> Your friends don't know you're
> here, right?

> TROY
> (beat)
> Right.
> (beat)
> Ms. Darbus is a little . . . harsh.

(CONTINUED)

                    GABRIELLA
          The Wildcat superstar is . . .
          afraid.

                     TROY
          Not afraid . . . just . . .
          (lets his guard down)
          . . . scared.

                    GABRIELLA
          (drops her guard, as well)
          Me too.
          (looking at Ms. Darbus)
          Hugely.

They both watch nervously from the
shadows.

BACK ON DARBUS - checking CLIPBOARD.

                    MS. DARBUS
          For the lead roles of Arnold and
          Minnie, we only have one couple
          signed up. Nevertheless, Ryan and
          Sharpay, I think it might be use-
          ful for you to give us a sense of
          why we gather in this hallowed
          hall.

RYAN and SHARPAY don't just walk on
stage, they make ENTRANCES from opposite sides of the stage. They bow as if

                                    (CONTINUED)

playing to Carnegie Hall, rather than
an empty auditorium. Sharpay GLARES at
Kelsi, who realizes she was supposed to
APPLAUD the entrance.

> KELSI
> (to Ryan) What key?

Ryan lifts a BOOM BOX.

> RYAN
> We had our rehearsal pianist do
> an arrangement.

MUSICAL NUMBER - SHARPAY AND RYAN -
UP-TEMPO

"WHAT I'VE BEEN LOOKING FOR" - by Adam
Watts & Andy Dodd

Ryan cues the music.

After the hack-a-rama we've witnessed at
least these two can SING. Their voices are
polished and their routine has clearly
been set by a professional choreographer.

> RYAN (CONT'D)
> *It's hard to believe*
> *That I couldn't see*

(CONTINUED)

                    BOTH
          You were always there beside me

When Ryan and Sharpay finish, if any of
the REMAINING KIDS were thinking about
auditioning at the last minute, they are
now fully intimidated and head for exits.

                    RYAN
          (to retreating students)
          Don't be discouraged. The theater
          club doesn't just need singers.
          It needs fans, too. Buy tickets!

KELSI, the young composer, slinks over
to Sharpay and Ryan.

                    KELSI
     (to Ryan and Sharpay, mustering courage)
          Actually, if you do the part
          with that particular song, I was
          hoping you'd--

                    SHARPAY
          If we do the part? Kelsi, my
          sawed-off Sondheim, I've been in
          seventeen school productions. And
          how many times have your compo-
          sitions been selected?

                    KELSI
          This would be the first.

                                    (CONTINUED)

                    SHARPAY
          Which tells us what?

                     KELSI
          That I need to write you more solos?

                    SHARPAY
          It tells us that you do not offer
          direction, suggestion, or commen-
          tary. And you should be thankful
          that me and Ryan are here to lift
          your music out of its current
          obscurity. Are we clear?

                    KELSI
                   Sir
          Yes, ma'am. I mean, Sharpay.

                    SHARPAY
          Nice talking to you.

Sharpay and Ryan exit.

Kelsi starts gathering her music.

                    MS. DARBUS
                  (to the room)
          Okay, we're out of time, so if we
          have any last-minute sign-ups?
          No? Good. Done.

Darbus tosses her clipboard into her
shoulder bag and starts to exit toward
the back of the house.
                                    (CONTINUED)

ON GABRIELLA - screws up her courage,
then runs to Ms. Darbus.

                    GABRIELLA
          I'd like to audition, Ms. Darbus.

                    MS. DARBUS
          Timeliness means something in the
          world of theater, young lady.
          Plus, the individual auditions
          are long, long over. And there
          were simply no other pairs.

Out of the darkness, we hear Troy's
voice-

                    TROY (O.S.)
          I'll sing with her.

Troy comes out of the shadows and
stands next to Gabriella, facing Ms.
Darbus.

                    MS. DARBUS
          Troy Bolton? Where is your sports
          posse or whatever it's called?

                    TROY
          Team. But I'm here alone. Actually--
            (indicates Gabriella)
          I'm here to sing with her.

                              (CONTINUED)

                    MS. DARBUS
          Yes, well, we take these shows
          very seriously here at East High.
          I called for the pairs audition,
          and you didn't respond.
                    (points to clock)
          --free period is now over. Next
          musical, perhaps.

Ms. Darbus heads for the back of the house.

ON KELSI - gathering her sheet music,
she turns and TRIPS over a piano leg.
She sprawls to the floor and sheets
scatter everywhere.

Troy hops up on stage, quickly lifts
Kelsi up from the ground, and helps her
collect the charts. Kelsi stares at him,
frozen. Troy Bolton has come to her aid.
The Troy Bolton? She's speechless.

                    TROY
          You composed the song that Ryan
          and Sharpay just sang?

Kelsi nods.

                 TROY (CONT'D)
          And the entire show?

                                        (CONTINUED)

Kelsi again can't get the words out, but
she nods.

> TROY (CONT'D)
> That's way cool. I can't wait to
> hear the rest of the show.

Kelsi just looks at him.

> TROY (CONT'D)
> Why are you so afraid of Ryan
> and Sharpay? I mean, it is your
> show.

> KELSI
> It is?

> TROY
> Isn't the composer of a show like
> the playmaker in basketball?

> KELSI
> Playmaker?

> TROY
> The person who makes everyone else
> look good. Without you, there
> is no show. You're the playmaker
> here, Kelsi.

Coming from Troy Bolton, these words im-
pact Kelsi.

(CONTINUED)

                    KELSI
    I am?
    (emboldened she sits at the piano,
      fumbles with her music)
    Do you wanna hear how the duet is
    supposed to sound?

She starts playing the AUDITION SONG
that Ryan and Sharpay rearranged.

                    Troy
    Wow, now that's really nice.

**MUSICAL NUMBER - GABRIELLA AND TROY -
(SLOW)**

"WHAT I'VE BEEN LOOKING FOR" - by Adam
Watts & Andy Dodd

Kelsi pushes music across the piano toward
Troy. He looks at it. Gabriella looks
at it, too.

TROY STARTS TO SING. Quietly, tentatively.

                TROY (CONT'D)
          It's hard to believe
          That I couldn't see
          You were always there beside me.

                              (CONTINUED)

Then GABRIELLA JOINS IN, a little bolder.

They are not trying to "perform," they
are just listening to Kelsi and soul-
fully interpreting the song.

Kelsi beams. It's the simple, pure version
of the music she'd been hoping to hear.
Like with the karaoke, Troy and Gabriella
gain confidence as the song progresses.
They sing truthfully, simply.

The song ends. Kelsi reacts with a look
of total appreciation.

NEW ANGLE - BACK OF THE HOUSE

MS. DARBUS stands in the darkness by
the back door, she's been watching,
listening.

                    MS. DARBUS
          (writes their names on a clipboard)
               Bolton, Montez - you have a call-
               back. Kelsi, give them the duet
               from the second act. Work on it
               with them.

THE BELL RINGS.

                                        (CONTINUED)

Troy and Gabriella look at each other . . . stunned . . . now what?

Kelsi HANDS THEM some SHEET MUSIC.

> KELSI
> If you guys want to rehearse, I'm usually in the music room during free period and after school, and even sometimes during biology class.

> > CUT TO:

EXT. SCHOOL - NEXT DAY

Full shot of the school. All is quiet. Then--

> SHARPAY (PRELAP)
> CALLBACK!!!

> > SMASH CUT:

INT. SCHOOL / MAIN HALLWAY - DAY

ON SHARPAY'S stunned, outraged expression.

(CONTINUED)

Sharpay and Ryan stand in front of the bulletin board where Ms. Darbus has posted the audition results.

> RYAN
> (reading the poster)
> Callback for roles Arnold and Minnie next Thursday, 3:30pm. Ryan and Sharpay Evans, Gabriella Montez and Troy Bolton.

> SHARPAY
> Is this some kind of joke? They didn't even audition!

> RYAN
> Maybe we're being punked?

> SHARPAY
> Shut up, Ryan!

A CROWD GATHERS . . . looking at the board.

Including CHAD, JASON, and ZEKE.

> CHAD
> (sees Troy's name on the list)
> WHAT?!?!?

CUT TO:

(CONTINUED)

INT. SCHOOL/CAFETERIA - SAME DAY

There's a large seating area. The VARIOUS
CLIQUES take their trays to usual tables . . .
Zeke, the jocks, Martha Cox, the brainiacs,
Sharpay, Ryan, the drama club, skater
dudes, cheerleaders, punks, etc.

ANGLE - DRAMA CLUB TABLE

Sharpay holds court at the head of the
DRAMA table. Half a dozen kids attend
~~her~~ every word, including RYAN and at
the far end, KELSI.

                    SHARPAY
          How dare she sign up! I've al-
          ready picked out the colors for
          my dressing room.

                    RYAN
          And she hasn't even asked our per-
          mission to join the drama club.

                    SHARPAY
          Someone's got to tell her the rules.

                    RYAN
          Exactly.
               (thinks about it)
          What are the rules?

                                    (CONTINUED)

Ryan's question transitions us to . . .

MUSICAL NUMBER - CAFETERIA. SHARPAY,
RYAN, ZEKE, SKATER DUDES, MARTHA COX,
STUDENT BODY

Gina's choreography is dazzling!!!!

"STICK TO THE STATUS QUO" - by David
and Fay Lawrence

ANGLE - THE PRIMO JOCK TABLE - TROY'S
BOYS

As the song climaxes, Gabriella STUM-
BLES and her TRAY GOES FLYING, spewing
CHILI FRIES, CATSUP, and melted CHEESE
all over . . . SHARPAY.

END OF SONG

Gabriella jumps up, beet red, and tries
to clean food from SHARPAY'S BLOUSE,
but it only makes it worse.

THE ENTIRE CAFETERIA IS FOCUSED ON
GABRIELLA AND SHARPAY.

NEW ANGLE - ON TROY . . . he enters the
cafeteria and SEES the COMMOTION between
Gabriella and SHARPAY.

(CONTINUED)

He heads toward their table, to help
Gabriella.

But CHAD INTERCEPTS HIM.

                    CHAD
          You can't get in the middle of
          that, Troy. Far too dangerous.

He drags Troy over to their usual table.
Troy NOTICES that everyone in the cafeteria
is BUZZING.

                    TROY
          What's up?

                    CHAD
          Oh, let's see . . . Umm, you
          missed free period workout yes-
          terday to audition for some
          heinous musical. Suddenly people
          are . . . confessing. Zeke is
          baking crème brûlée.

                    TROY
          Ah, what's that?

                    ZEKE
          A creamy custard-like filling
          with a caramelized surface. Very
          satisfying.

                              (CONTINUED)

                    CHAD
          Shut up, Zeke!
               (to Troy)

          Do you see what's happening? Our
          team is coming apart because of
          your singing thing. Even the drama
          geeks and the brainiacs suddenly
          think that they can . . . talk to
          us. The skater dudes are mingling.
          People think they can suddenly . . .
          do other stuff. Stuff that is
          not their stuff.
          (points to the kids at Sharpay's
          DRAMA CLUB TABLE. To Troy-)
             They've got you thinking about
             show tunes, when we've got a
             playoff game next week.

     MS. DARBUS passes through the cafeteria.
     She takes in the chaos of all the various
     student groups in turmoil. She approaches
     SHARPAY, who is cleaning her blouse
     with a napkin.

                 MS. DARBUS
          What happened here?

                  SHARPAY
          Look at this! That Gabriella
          girl dumped her lunch on me . . .

                                  (CONTINUED)

on purpose! It's all part of
their plan to ruin our musical.
(indicates jock table)
And Troy and his basketball robots
are obviously behind it. Why do
you think he auditioned? After
all the work you've put into this
show, it just doesn't seem right.

Angle on KELSI . . . watching Sharpay
work Ms. Darbus.

INT. COACHES OFFICE - MOMENTS LATER

Troy's dad, COACH BOLTON, eats his
lunch and reads the sports section of
the newspaper.

MS. DARBUS confronts him.

             MS. DARBUS
        All right, Bolton, cards on the
        table right now.

             COACH BOLTON
        Huh?

             MS. DARBUS
        You're tweaked because I put your
        stars in detention and now you're
        getting even?

                                    (CONTINUED)

COACH BOLTON
What are you talking about, Darbus?

MS. DARBUS
Your all-star son turned up at
my audition. I give every student
an even chance, which is a long
and honorable tradition in the
theater--something you wouldn't
understand--but, if he's planning some kind of practical joke
in my chapel of the arts--

COACH BOLTON
Troy doesn't even sing.

MS. DARBUS
Oh, you're wrong about that. But
I won't allow my "Twinkle Town"
musical to be made into a farce--

COACH BOLTON
(stifles a laugh)
--"Twinkle Town"?

MS. DARBUS
See? I knew it! I knew it!

INT. SCHOOL / CAFETERIA - DAY

Taylor and Gabriella eye the turmoil at
Sharpay's table.

(CONTINUED)

GABRIELLA

Is Sharpay really, really mad at
me? I said I was sorry.

TAYLOR

No one has beaten out Sharpay for
a musical since kindergarten.

GABRIELLA

I'm not trying to beat anyone
out. We weren't even auditioning.
We were just singing.

TAYLOR

You won't convince Sharpay of
that. If that girl guy could figure
out a way to play both Romeo and
Juliet, her own brother would be
aced out of a job.

GABRIELLA

I told you it just . . .
happened. But I liked it. A lot.
          (beat)
Did you ever feel like there's
this whole other person inside
of you just looking for a way to
come out?

TAYLOR

No.

(CONTINUED)

THE LUNCH PERIOD ENDING BELL RINGS.

Angle - students file out. SHARPAY
sends a death-ray glance in Gabriella's
direction.
ZEKE steps in front of SHARPAY.

                    ZEKE
          Hey, Sharpay. Now that Troy's
          going to be in your show . . .

                    SHARPAY
               (holding her finger up)
          Troy Bolton is <u>not</u> in my show!

DELETE SCENE   ZEKE
          I thought maybe you'd like to
          come to see me play ball some-
          time--

                    SHARPAY
          I'd rather stick pins in my eyes.

                    ZEKE
          Wouldn't that be awfully uncom-
          fortable?

                    SHARPAY
          Evaporate, tall person!

          He
          ~~She~~ storms away.

                              (CONTINUED)

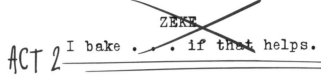

ZEKE

I bake . . . if that helps.

ACT 2

INT. SCHOOL / CHEM HALLWAY - GABRIELLA'S
LOCKER - DAY

She opens her locker. FINDS A NOTE.
Reads it.

On Gabriella's face . . . she's confused,
intrigued.

INT. SCHOOL/ UPPER-FLOOR HALLWAY -
CONTINUOUS

Gabriella glances at the NOTE she found
in her locker, then SEES a YELLOW door at
the end of the hall . . . beelines for it.

EXT. SCHOOL / ROOFTOP GARDEN - MOMENTS
LATER

Troy is surrounded by a bunch of plants,
courtesy of the horticulture club.

A door opens, Gabriella pokes her head
out, sees Troy.

                    GABRIELLA
          (indicates rooftop garden)
          So this is your private hideout?

                              (CONTINUED)

                    TROY
        (points to the hydroponic experiments)
              Thanks to the science club. Which
              means that my buddies don't even
              know about it.

                  GABRIELLA
              Looks like everyone on campus
              wants to be your friend.

                    TROY
              Unless we lose.

                  GABRIELLA
              I'm sure it's tricky being the
              coach's son.

                    TROY
              It makes me practice a little
              harder, I guess. I don't know
              what he'll say when he hears about
              the singing thing.

                  GABRIELLA
              You're worried?

                    TROY
              My parents' friends are always
              saying, "Your son's the basket-
              ball guy, you must be so proud."
              Sometimes I don't want be "the
              basketball guy." I just want to
              be a guy.

                                    (CONTINUED)

                    GABRIELLA
I saw the way you treated Kelsi at
the audition yesterday. Do your
friends know that guy?

                    TROY
To them, I'm the playmaker dude.

                    GABRIELLA
Then they don't know enough about
you, Troy.
                    (beat)
At my other schools I was the
"freaky math girl." It's cool
coming here and being . . . anyone
I want to be. When I was singing
with you I just felt like . . .
a girl.

                    TROY
You even look like one, too.

She laughs.

                    GABRIELLA
Remember in kindergarten you'd
meet a kid, know nothing about
them, then ten seconds later were
best friends, because you didn't
have to be anything but yourself?

                                            (CONTINUED)

                    TROY
          Yeah . . .

                  GABRIELLA
          Singing with you felt like that.

                    TROY
          I never thought about singing,
          that's for sure. Until you.

                  GABRIELLA
          So you really want to do the
          callbacks?

                    TROY
          (thinks about it, really looks at
               her . . . then--)
          Hey, just call me "freaky call-
          back boy."

That brings a smile to Gabriella's face.

                  GABRIELLA
          You're a cool guy, Troy. But not
          for the reasons your friends think.

Troy shuffles around.

               GABRIELLA (CONT'D)
          Thanks for showing me your
          top-secret hiding place. Like
          kindergarten.

                                        (CONTINUED)

THE BELL RINGS.

ON TROY'S FACE . . . realizes he's LATE,
and he knows that means DETENTION.

CUT TO:

DELETE SCENE

REHEARSAL MONTAGE - TROY, GABRIELLA,
KELSI

"BREAKING FREE (SCORE VERSION)" - by
Jamie Houston

INT. REHEARSAL ROOM - NEXT DAY

Kelsi sits alone at her piano, with her
music. Here, we see her passion, her true
personality, as she plays alone with
all her heart . . . to an empty room.
The music carries us to--

INT. SCHOOL / STAIRWELL - DAY

Troy sits by himself, practicing Kelsi's
audition song. Pan down to classroom
BELOW.

(CONTINUED)

                    TROY
          You know the world can see us
          In a way that's different than
          who we are

INT. SCHOOL / HALLWAY - DAY

Ryan rounds a corner in the hall and
thinks he hears singing.

INT. SCHOOL / GIRLS' BATHROOM - DAY

Three girls leave.

New angles - GABRIELLA alone in front of
the mirror. SINGING the audition song.

                  GABRIELLA
          Creating space between us
          Till we're separate hearts

EXT. SCHOOL / CHEM HALLWAY - SAME TIME

Sharpay heading for class. HEARS
SINGING . . . he thinks. Opens the
BATHROOM DOOR. Gabriella hides herself.
Sharpay thinks he must have been
hearing things.

                              (CONTINUED)

INT. SCHOOL / REHEARSAL ROOM - DAY

Kelsi at the piano, playing for Gabriella,
helping her with her phrasing.

INT. SCHOOL / REHEARSAL ROOM - DAY

Now it's Troy's turn to work with Kelsi.
Troy looks a little frustrated, but
Kelsi is all about encouragement.

INT. SCHOOL / GYM - DAY

DELETE
MONTAGE

The players warm up for practice.

COACH BOLTON looks at the CLOCK.

No Troy.

The CLOCK transitions us to--

INT. SCHOOL / THEATER - STAGE - DAY

Troy and Gabriella stand on opposite
sides of the stage, painting scenery,
stealing glances at one another. From
the looks on their faces we know they
are hearing the song in their heads.

MS. DARBUS eyeballs them.

(CONTINUED)

INT. SCHOOL / GYM - LATER

Troy races into the gym where his team
and coach are waiting.

INT. SCHOOL / GYM - LATER SAME DAY

Basketball practice ends, the players
head for the locker room. All except
Troy.

> TROY
> (to his father)
> I'm going to stay a while, work
> on free throws.

> COACH BOLTON
> Since you were late for practice . . .
> again . . . I think your team-
> mates deserve a little extra effort
> from you.

He gives Troy a look, and heads for the
coach's room.

Troy begins shooting in the empty gym.

GABRIELLA pokes her head in through one
of the doors. Troy waves her in.

(CONTINUED)

                    GABRIELLA
                 (looking around)
        Wow. So this is your . . . real
        stage.

                      TROY
        I guess you could call it that.
        Or just a smelly gym.

He bounces the ball to her.

She takes a shot. Not bad.

                      TROY
        Whoa . . . don't tell me your
        good at hoops, too.

                    GABRIELLA
        I once scored forty-one points in
        a league championship game.

                      TROY
        No way.

                    GABRIELLA
        Yeah . . . the same day I invented
        the space shuttle and microwave
        popcorn.

He laughs, steals the ball back from
her. Takes a shot. Gabriella rebounds
the miss.

                              (CONTINUED)

                    GABRIELLA (CONT'D)
          I've been rehearsing with Kelsi.

                         TROY
          I know. Me too. And I was late
          for practice. So if I get kicked
          off the team it should be on your
          conscience.

                       GABRIELLA
          Hey, I--

                         TROY
                    (he's kidding)
          Gabriella, chill.

          She gives him a look, and bounces the
          ball back to him.

                    COACH BOLTON (O.S.)
               (voice booms in the gym)
          Miss, I'm sorry, this is a closed
          practice.

          Coach Bolton strides back into the gym.

                         TROY
          Dad, practice is over.

                      COACH BOLTON
          Not till the last player leaves
          the gym. Team rule.

                                        (CONTINUED)

                    GABRIELLA
          Oh, I'm sorry, sir.

                      TROY
          Dad, this is Gabriella Montez.

                  COACH BOLTON
          Your detention buddy?

                    GABRIELLA
          I'll see you later, Troy. Nice
          meeting you, Coach Bolton.

                  COACH BOLTON
          You as well, Miss Montez.

Gives her a stern look. She makes a
hasty exit.

Troy faces his dad.

                      TROY
          Detention was my fault, not hers.

                  COACH BOLTON
          You haven't missed practice in
          three years. That girl turns up
          and you're late twice.

                      TROY
          "That girl" is named Gabriella.
          And she's very nice.

                                      (CONTINUED)

                    COACH BOLTON
Helping you miss practice doesn't
make her "very nice." Not in my
book. Or your team's.

                    TROY
She's not a problem, Dad, she's
just . . . a girl.

                    COACH BOLTON
You're not just "a guy," Troy.
You're the team leader. What you
do affects not only this team,
but the entire school. Without
you completely focused, we won't
win next week. And playoff games
don't come along all the time . . .
they're something special.

                    TROY
A lot of things are special.

                    COACH BOLTON
You're a playmaker, not a singer.

                    TROY
Did you ever think maybe I could
be both?

Troy heads for the locker room. His dad
watches him.

                                    (CONTINUED)

ADD SCENE: Ms. Darbus approaches Coach Bolton and Troy.

> MS. DARBUS
> And I expect to see you back in detention pronto to prepare for the musical, young man.

> COACH BOLTON
> East High is all about basketball, not dance numbers. If you wanted to do theater, you should have stayed in New York, Ms. Darbus.

Ms. Darbus walks back to her classroom. She sings power ballad "Wondering."

INT. SCHOOL / LOCKER ROOM - SAME TIME

Chad, Jason, and Zeke are all huddled in the small transition hallway between the locker room and gym. They have the DOOR to the GYM open a crack.

They've WATCHED and LISTENED to the entire exchange between TROY and his DAD.

DELETE SCENE

FADE TO:

INT. SCHOOL / LIBRARY - NEXT DAY

(CONTINUED)

Chad is next to TROY at a study table.

                    CHAD
          What spell has this elevated-IQ
          temptress girl cast that suddenly
          makes you want to be in a musi-
          cal?

                    TROY
          I just . . . did it. Who cares?

                    CHAD
          Who cares? How about your most
          loyal best friend?

                    LIBRARIAN
          Quiet in here, Mr. Danforth.

                    CHAD
               (points to Troy)
          It's him, Miss Falstaff, not me.

The librarian passes by.

                    CHAD (CONT'D)
          You're a hoops dude, not a musical
          singer person. ~~Have you ever seen~~
          ~~Michael Crawford on a cereal box?~~

                    ~~TROY~~
          ~~Who's Michael Crawford?~~

                                    (CONTINUED)

CHAD

Exactly my point. He was the
Phantom of the Opera on Broadway. My mom saw that musical
twenty-seven times, and put
Michael Crawford's picture in
our refrigerator. Not on it, _in
it_. Play basketball, you end up
on a cereal box. Sing in musi-
cals, you end up in my mom's
refrigerator.

DELETE

TROY

Why would she put his picture in
her refrigerator?

CHAD

One of her crazy diet ideas. I do
not attempt to understand the female
mind, Troy. That's frightening
territory.

~~The LIBRARIAN is approaching again.~~

CHAD (CONT'D)
(whispers)

How can you expect the rest of us
to be focused on a game if you're
off somewhere in leotards singing
in "Twinkle Town"?

(CONTINUED)

                    TROY
          No one said anything about leo-
          tards . . .

                    CHAD
          . . . maybe not yet, my friend,
          but just you wait! We need you,
          Captain. Big time.

                  LIBRARIAN
          Mr. Danforth.

                    CHAD
          I've tried to tell him, Miss
          Falstaff.
                    (to Troy)
          I've really tried.

Chad slinks away, under the glaring eye
of the librarian.

Troy sits there, thinking about what
Chad said.

INT. SCHOOL / CHEMISTRY LAB - SAME DAY
- LATER

Tables full of test tubes, petri dishes,
and ongoing experiments. TAYLOR and the
scholastic girls are hard at work. The
clock behind them reads 3:20.

                              (CONTINUED)

CHAD, JASON and ZEKE ENTER THE LAB and
look around. They are strangers in a
strange land.

                    CHAD
          We need to talk.

                              CUT TO:

INT. SCHOOL / CHEM HALLWAY - CONTINUOUS

SHARPAY and RYAN pass the CHEM LAB, and
NOTICE CHAD and the JOCKS conferring
with TAYLOR and the Scholastic Club.
They pause to spy on them.

                  SHARPAY
          Something isn't right.

                   RYAN
          They must be trying to figure
          out a way to make sure Troy and
          Gabriella actually beat us out.
          The jocks rule most of the school,
          but if they get Troy into the
          musical, then they've conquered
          the entire student body.

                              (CONTINUED)

SHARPAY

And if those science girls get Gabriella hooked up with Troy Bolton, the Scholastic Club goes from drool to cool.
(this is war)
Ryan, we need to save our show from people who don't know the difference between a Tony Award and Tony Hawk.

CUT TO:

INT. SCHOOL / CHEMISTRY LAB - CONTINUOUS

Chad has obviously pitched an idea to the Scholastic Club crowd. A lot of DUBIOUS LOOKS from his fellow students.

TAYLOR

You really think that's going to work?

CHAD

It's the only way to save Troy and Gabriella from themselves.

Taylor looks at her team.

(CONTINUED)

After a brief hesitation, THEY NOD in
unison.

                    CHAD (CONT'D)
            We start tomorrow.

                                    FADE TO:
DELETE SCENE

EXT. SCHOOL COURTYARD - NEXT DAY -
MORNING

Kids arriving on the way to class.

ON CHAD, looks around, as if he's on a
secret mission.

SEES TAYLOR across the quad, gives her
a NOD.

She rolls her eyes, and meets him over in
a CORNER.

                    CHAD
            My watch says 7:45 Central Stan-
            dard Time. Are we synched?

                    TAYLOR
            (doesn't wear a watch)
            Whatever.

                                    (CONTINUED)

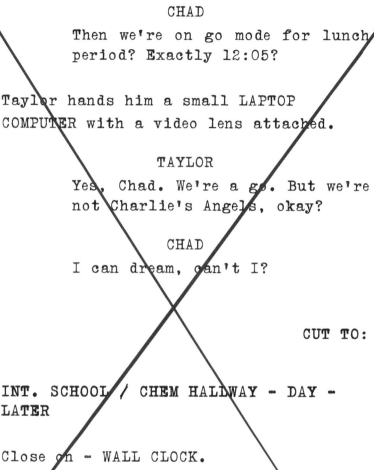

                    CHAD
          Then we're on go mode for lunch
          period? Exactly 12:05?

Taylor hands him a small LAPTOP
COMPUTER with a video lens attached.

                    TAYLOR
          Yes, Chad. We're a go. But we're
          not Charlie's Angels, okay?

                    CHAD
          I can dream, can't I?

                                        CUT TO:

INT. SCHOOL / CHEM HALLWAY - DAY -
LATER

Close on - WALL CLOCK.
Exactly 12:05.

BELL RINGS. Students head for lunch.

Locker room set at stage right

INT. SCHOOL / LOCKER ROOM - DAY

Troy enters the locker room and heads
for the TEAM ROOM. When he arrives, his
ENTIRE TEAM is already there, waiting

                              (CONTINUED)

for him. As soon as Troy enters, JASON
closes the door and blocks it.

In the center of the room is CHAD,
standing next to a table of TROPHIES
and PHOTOS. Before Troy can say a word,
CHAD picks up the first PHOTO.

                    CHAD
          "Spider" Bill Natrine, class of
          '99. MVP, league championship game.

Chad POINTS TO A TROPHY.

Zeke holds up the next PHOTO.

                    ZEKE
          Sam Netletter, class of '02.
          Known far and wide as "Sammy
          Slamma-Jamma."   Captain,   MVP,
          league championship team.

Zeke POINTS TO A TROPHY.

Jason holds up the next PHOTO.

                    JASON
          Thunderclap Hap Haddon, '95.

POINTS to TWO TROPHIES.

(CONTINUED)

                    JASON (CONT'D)
Led the Wildcats to back-to-back
city championships. A legend.

                    CHAD
Yes, legends, one and all. And
do you think that any of these
Wildcat legends became legends
by getting involved in musical
auditions, just days before the
league championship playoffs?

                    TEAM
Getcha head in the game!

                    CHAD
These Wildcat legends became legends because they never took their
eye off the prize.

                    TEAM
Getcha head in the game!

                    CHAD
                    (to team)
Now, who was the first sophomore
ever to make starting varsity?

                    TROY'S BOYS
Troy!

                              (CONTINUED)

                    CHAD
So, who voted him our team captain
this year?

                  TROY'S BOYS
Us!

                    CHAD
And who is going to get their
sorry butts kicked in Friday's
championship game if Troy's worried
about an audition?

                  WILDCATS
                 (depressed)
We are.

                    TROY
Hey, there are twelve of us on
this team. Not just me.

                    CHAD
Just twelve? I think you're
forgetting a very important thir-
teenth member of our squad--

CHAD pulls out ANOTHER PHOTO.

An eight-by-ten black and white of
a kid in a BASKETBALL UNIFORM . . .
from the UNIFORM and HAIRSTYLE, this
one obviously is an OLDIE.

                        (CONTINUED)

Looking at the PHOTO, TROY'S JAW DROPS.

                    TROY
                  (realizes)
          That's my dad.

Chad props the PHOTO against an old
TROPHY.

                    CHAD
          Yes, Troy, Wildcat basketball
          champion, class of 1981. Champion,
          father, and now coach. It's a
          winning tradition like no other.

Troy can't believe what's happening.

Chem Room set at Stage Left

INT. SCHOOL / CHEMISTRY LAB - SAME TIME

The brainiac girls are assembled. Gabriella
sits in the midst of them. They've
BROWN-BAGGED their lunches. TAYLOR is
at the dry-erase board, using a LASER
POINTER. There are sequential PHOTOS
and SKETCHES depicting EVOLUTION.

                    TAYLOR
          From   lowly   Neanderthal   and
          Cro-Magnon, to early warriors,
          medieval knights. All leading up
          to . . .

                                      (CONTINUED)

(unscrolls full-length photo
of basketball player's BODY,
with Troy Bolton's HEAD)
. . . lunkhead basketball man!

Yes, our culture worshipped the
aggressor throughout the ages and
we end up with spoiled, overpaid,
bonehead athletes who contribute
little to civilization other
than slam dunks and touchdowns.
That is the inevitable world of
Troy Bolton.

Taylor goes to another wall.

                    TAYLOR (CONT'D)
But the path of the mind, the path
we're on, ours is the path that
has brought us these people--

Photos of--

Eleanor Roosevelt, Frida Kahlo,
Sandra Day O'Connor, Madame Cu-
rie, Jane Goodall, Oprah Winfrey,
and so many others who the world
reveres.

                    GABRIELLA
But what has this . . . I've got
Kelsi waiting for me to rehearse.

                                        (CONTINUED)

TAYLOR

Gabriella, Troy Bolton represents one side of evolution . . . lunkhead basketball man. And our side, the side of education and accomplishment, is the future of civilization! That's the side where you belong.

CUT BACK TO:

INT. SCHOOL / TEAM ROOM - SAME TIME - CONTINUOUS

TROY
(to team)
If you don't know that I'll put one hundred and ten percent of my guts into that game, then you don't know me.

CHAD
Well, we just thought--

TROY
I'll tell you what I thought. I thought that you're my friends. Win together, lose together, teammates.

(CONTINUED)

                    CHAD
          But suddenly the girl and the
          singing--

NEW ANGLE - CHAD stands next to THE
LAPTOP that TAYLOR GAVE HIM, with its
video-link CAMERA mounted on it . . .

                    TROY
             (they've worn him down)
          I'm for the team! I've always been
          for the team. She's just someone
          I met.

THE LAPTOP CAMERA IS TRANSMITTING A LIVE
FEED TO--

INT. SCHOOL / CHEMISTRY LAB - SAME TIME

                    TROY
             (on laptop screen)
          . . . the singing thing is noth-
          ing. Probably just a way to keep
          my nerves down. I don't know.
          It doesn't mean anything to me.
          You're my guys and this is our
          team. Gabriella's not important.
          I'll forget about her, I'll forget
          the audition, and we'll go out and
          get that championship. Everyone
          happy now?

                                    (CONTINUED)

Taylor indicates COMPUTER SCREEN.

They've frozen it on an image of TROY.

                    TAYLOR
          Behold lunkhead basketball man.
              (looks at Gabriella)
          So, Gabriella, we'd love to have
          you for the Scholastic Decathlon.

The girls awkwardly shuffle toward the door.

All except for GABRIELLA. She stays behind.

                    TAYLOR (CONT'D)
          Do you want to grab some lunch?

Gabriella shakes her head. Wants to be alone.
Taylor leaves. Now the room is empty.
Gabriella HEARS some noise coming from
the QUAD below. her POV from window--

EXT. FIELD - SAME TIME

There is an impromptu pep rally that
popped up at lunch and is traveling
across the quad. We see drummers, cheerleaders, other kids with BANNERS. Kids
CHANTING for a Wildcat victory. The

(CONTINUED)

basketball team swarm TROY, trying to
pump him up. *Talk to Carlos re: his Forest of Boys choreography. Not sure it will work!*

INT. SCHOOL / CHEMISTRY LAB - SAME TIME

MUSICAL NUMBER - GABRIELLA - EMPTY HALLS

"WHEN THERE WAS ME AND YOU" - by Jamie
Houston

She turns away from the window and begins
to sing. *STAGING IDEA: Gabriella sings as she walks down hall. Use scrolling lockers!*

> GABRIELLA
> *It's funny when you find yourself*
> *Looking from the outside*
> *I'm standing here*
> *But all I want is to be over there*

She exits the chem lab . . .

INT SCHOOL / HALLWAY - CONTINUOUS

. . . and continues the song as she walks
down the empty hallways of East High.

The spirit of Troy and the Wildcats
seems to be everywhere; trophy cases,
banners, murals . . . it's inescapable.

(CONTINUED)

She descends a staircase winding down
to another floor.

She exits a stairwell and moves past an
ENORMOUS, LARGER-THAN-LIFE mural of the
Wildcats team featuring TROY, his baby
blues staring out at her.

INT. SCHOOL / CHEM HALLWAY - LOCKERS -
DAY

On Gabriella, putting things in her
LOCKER.

TROY approaches her.

>   TROY
>   Hey, how you doin'?

She doesn't look at him.

>   TROY (CONT'D)
>   Listen, there's something I need
>   to talk to you about, okay?

>   GABRIELLA
>   And here it is: I know what it's
>   like to carry a load with your
>   friends. I get it. You've got
>   your boys, Troy. It's okay. So
>   we're good.

                              (CONTINUED)

                    TROY
          Good about what? I need to talk
          to you about the final callbacks.

                  GABRIELLA
          I don't want to do the callbacks,
          either. Who   are   we   kidding?
          You've got your team and now I've
          got mine. I'll do the Scholastic
          Decathlon and you'll win the cham-
          pionships. It's where we belong. Go
          Wildcats.

She pulls SHEET MUSIC from her locker.

                    TROY
          But I don't . . .

                  GABRIELLA
          Me either.

She HANDS HIM THE SHEET MUSIC, and
WALKS AWAY.

Troy calls after her, but Gabriella
DOESN'T RESPOND.

Bell RINGS. Next class.

                              FADE TO:

                              (CONTINUED)

MONTAGE - TROY AND GABRIELLA - VARIOUS DAYS

DELETE SCENE

Music over various shots.

EXT. SCHOOL / TRACK - DAY

P.E. Class OUTSIDE. Chad, Jason, and Zeke and two other players doing a Harlem Globetrotter's-style circle passing routine. They wave at TROY to come over. Troy ignores them. CHAD STARTS WALKING TOWARD HIM, but Troy heads for a jog.

EXT. BOLTON HOUSE / BACKYARD - EVENING

Troy shooting hoops at night.

Angle - his DAD watches from the kitchen.

Knows something is up, but also knows it's not the time to push.

INT. MONTEZ HOUSE / GABRIELLA'S BED-ROOM - EVENING

She sits on her small balcony off the bedroom. Books are spread around. But she's not reading. She's just look-

(CONTINUED)

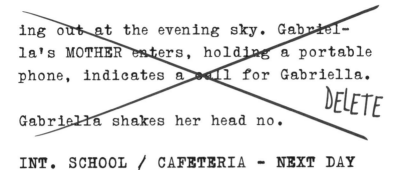

INT. SCHOOL / CAFETERIA - NEXT DAY

Troy and Gabriella happen to pass each
other with trays.

There is an awkward moment, but then
each just keeps going without exchanging a word.

NEW ANGLE - ON CHAD, who glances over
at TAYLOR.

They BOTH SAW what just happened.

Chad nods, so does Taylor . . . they've
seen enough. They know they really
screwed up.

End montage.

CUT TO:

EXT. SCHOOL / ROOFTOP GARDEN - DAY

Troy's by himself and CHAD appears,
followed by ZEKE and JASON.

             CHAD
      We just had another team meeting,
      Troy.

             TROY
      Wonderful.

             CHAD
      We had a team meeting about how we
      haven't been acting like a team.
      Us, not you. The singing thing--

             TROY
      I don't even want to talk about it.

             CHAD
      We just want you to know that we're
      gonna be there cheering for you.

             TROY
      Huh?

             ZEKE
      Yeah, Cap, if singing is some-
      thing you want to do, we should
      be boosting you up, not tearing
      you down.

                              (CONTINUED)

                    CHAD
          Win or lose, we're teammates.
          That's what we're about. Even
          if you turn out to be the worst
          singer in the world--

                    JASON
          --which we don't know because we
          haven't actually heard you sing.

                    TROY
          And you're not going to hear me
          sing, dudes, because Gabriella
          won't even talk to me . . . and I
          don't know why.

                    CHAD
                    (beat)
          We do.

Zeke pulls a bag of COOKIES from his
backpack.

                    ZEKE
          Baked these fresh today. Want to
          try one before we tell you the
          rest?

                              CUT TO:

                         (CONTINUED)

INT. SCHOOL / CHEMISTRY LAB - SAME TIME

Gabriella is surrounded by Taylor and
the scholastic girls.

> TAYLOR
> We're worse than jerks because
> we're mean jerks. We thought Troy
> and the whole singing thing was
> killing our chances of having you
> on the Scholastic Decathlon team.

> GABRIELLA
> Why talk about it? I heard what
> he had to say. I'm on your team
> now. Done.

> TAYLOR
> No, not done.
> (beat)
> Chad knew he could get Troy to say
> things that would make you want
> to forget about the callbacks. We
> planned it. We're embarrassed and
> sorry.

> GABRIELLA
> (putting on a good front)
> No one forced Troy to say any-
> thing. And you know what? It's
> okay. We should be preparing for
> the Decathlon now. So it's time
> to move on.

(CONTINUED)

> TAYLOR
>
> No, it's not. The Scholastic De-
> cathlon is . . . whatever. How you
> feel about us, and Troy, that's
> something else.

CUT TO:

DELETE SCENE

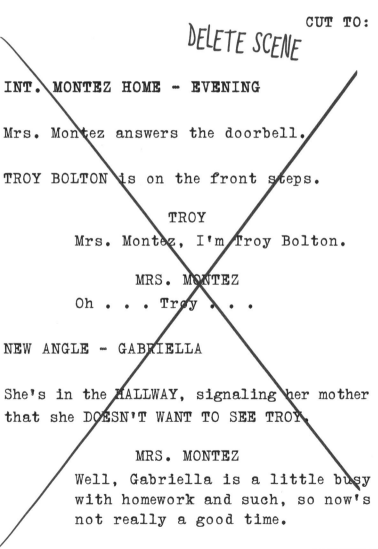

INT. MONTEZ HOME - EVENING

Mrs. Montez answers the doorbell.

TROY BOLTON is on the front steps.

> TROY
>
> Mrs. Montez, I'm Troy Bolton.

> MRS. MONTEZ
>
> Oh . . . Troy . . .

NEW ANGLE - GABRIELLA

She's in the HALLWAY, signaling her mother
that she DOESN'T WANT TO SEE TROY.

> MRS. MONTEZ
>
> Well, Gabriella is a little busy
> with homework and such, so now's
> not really a good time.

(CONTINUED)

                    TROY
~~I made a mistake, Mrs. Montez,
and I need to let Gabriella know
that. Could you tell her that I
came by to see her?~~

DELETE

                    MRS. MONTEZ
                    (smiling)
     I will . . . Troy. Good night.

EXT. MONTEZ HOME - SECONDS LATER

Troy crosses the lawn. Notices a BED-
ROOM LIGHT get switched on at the far
end of the SECOND STORY. THERE is a
small BALCONY outside the room. Troy
takes out his CELL PHONE, punches in
Gabriella's number.

**INT. MONTEZ HOME / GABRIELLA'S BED-
ROOM - SAME TIME**

GABRIELLA in her ROOM.

Sees Troy's photo come up on her cell
phone screen. Thinks about it. Finally
she answers.

INTERCUT PHONE CALL

                                    (CONTINUED)

                    TROY
              (into cell phone)
        What you heard, none of that is
        true. I was sick of my friends
        riding me about singing with you,
        and I said things I knew would
        shut them up. I didn't mean any
        of it.

Gabriella turns on her nightstand lamp.

                  GABRIELLA
              (on the phone)
        You sounded pretty convincing to
        me.

ON TROY

He SEES Gabriella moving about in her
room.

He looks up to the BALCONY.

Then he sees a TREE and STARTS CLIMBING.

                    TROY
              (into phone)
        The guy you met on vacation is
        way more me than the guy who said
        those stupid things.

                                    (CONTINUED)

                    GABRIELLA
                   (into phone)
          Troy, the whole singing thing is
          making the school whack. You said
          so yourself. Everyone's treating
          you differently because of it.

                    TROY
                   (into phone)
          Maybe because I don't want to only
          be "the basketball guy" anymore.
          They can't handle it. That's not
          my problem, it's theirs.

Troy makes it up to the BALCONY.

Gabriella is just a few feet away, her
back to him, unaware of his presence.

                    GABRIELLA
                   (into phone)
          What about your dad--

                    TROY
                   (into phone)
          This isn't about my dad. This
          is about how I feel, and I'm not
          letting the team down. They let
          me down. So I'm going to sing.
          What about you?

                                        (CONTINUED)

                    GABRIELLA
                  (into phone)
        I don't know, Troy.

                      TROY
                  (into phone)
        You need to say yes. Because I
        brought something for you.

                    GABRIELLA
                  (into phone)
        What do you mean?

Troy lowers his phone.

MUSICAL NUMBER - TROY

"SOMETHING NEW (REPRISE)" - by Matthew
Gerrard & Robbie Nevil

Gabriella turns around and there's Troy
STANDING ON HER BALCONY. He sings a
cappella, ballad style.

                      TROY
              Start of something new
              It feels so right to be here
              with you

She is stunned . . . but happy. Troy
smiles.

                                    (CONTINUED)

TROY (CONT'D)
It's a pairs audition.

He hands her the SHEET MUSIC she'd given back to him.

They look at each other. The smile grows on Gabriella's face.

FADE TO:

DELETE MONTAGE

MONTAGE - TROY AND GABRIELLA - MOS

INT. SCHOOL / GYM - NEXT DAY

Various shots.

Troy running his team.

Back on his game. Top of his form.

INT. SCHOOL / CHEMISTRY LAB - DAY

Various shots.

Gabriella at dry-erase board, running formulas, briefing her team. Focused and impressive.

(CONTINUED)

DELETE MONTAGE

INT. SCHOOL - HALLWAY - DAY

Various shots.

Troy runs out of the locker room after practice.

Gabriella comes flying out of the chem lab.

They meet on the run and go to---

INT. REHEARSAL ROOM - DAY

Troy and Gabriella rehearsing with Kelsi.

End montage.

INT. SCHOOL / HALLWAY - REHEARSAL ROOM - DAY

Sharpay and Ryan come out of their own rehearsal and hear Gabriella and Troy's singing.

                    RYAN
          Wow, they sound good.

                                    (CONTINUED)

                    SHARPAY
                (wheels are turning)
            We have to do something. Our callback
            is on Thursday, the basketball
            game and the Scholastic Decathlon
            are on Friday. Too bad all these
            events weren't happening on the
            same day at the same time.

                    RYAN
            Well, that wouldn't work out because
            then Troy and Gabriella wouldn't
            be able to make the callback.
        (off Sharpay's purposeful look . . .
                    eureka!)
            I'm proud to call you my brother ~~sister.~~

INT. SCHOOL / THEATER - DAY

Ryan and Sharpay are with Ms. Darbus.

                    MS. DARBUS
            So if you're telling me, as
            co-presidents of the drama club,
            that changing the callbacks would
            be what's best for our theater
            program, then I might actually
            agree with you.

Ms. Darbus gives them a look, and walks
away.

                                    (CONTINUED)

Ryan scratches his head.

                    RYAN
                (to Sharpay)
        Was that a yes?

SHARPAY gives ~~her~~ his brother a "mission
accomplished" WINK.

NEW ANGLE - KELSI

The young composer witnessed the entire
exchange.

Including the WINK.

                                FADE TO:

INT. SCHOOL / MAIN HALLWAY - BULLETIN
BOARD - NEXT DAY

TROY and GABRIELLA arrive at school
early to meet up with Kelsi. But they
FIND KELSI standing in front of the
bulletin board, with an ashen look on
her face.

Close on - SIGN

                                (CONTINUED)

"MUSICAL AUDITIONS RESCHEDULED TO FRIDAY 3:30 PM"

Troy and Gabriella stare glumly at the sign.

                    TROY
          Same time as the game--

                  GABRIELLA
          And the Scholastic Decathlon--

CHAD and TAYLOR and their respective "teams" converge behind Troy and Gabriella at the board.

                   TAYLOR
          Well, I just don't know why they
          would do that.

                    CHAD
          I smell a rat named Darbus.

                 KELSI (O.S.)
          Actually, I think it's two rats,
          neither of them named Darbus.

Everyone turns. Kelsi is almost lost amid the tall-tree basketball players.

                                        (CONTINUED)

                         CHAD
          Do you know something about this,
          small person?

                         KELSI
          Ms. Darbus might think that
          she's protecting the show, but
          Ryan and Sharpay are pretty much
          only concerned with protecting
          themselves.

                         CHAD
          Do you know what I'm going to do
          to those two over-moussed show
          dogs--

                         TROY
                   (takes command)
          Nothing. We're not going to do
          anything to them. Except sing,
          maybe.

Everyone looks at Troy.

                    TROY (CONT'D)
               (looks at both basketball team
                  and scholastic club)
              --this is only going to happen
              if we all work together. Who's in?

The teams eyeball each other. CHAD holds
up a HAND and TAYLOR high-fives it.

                              (CONTINUED)

FADE TO:

INT. SCHOOL / HOMEROOM - ANOTHER DAY

Chad and the boys present Taylor with a
CAKE baked by Zeke:

Icing reads:

   Scholastic Decathalon Today - Support
           Brain Fame!

Taylor and her girls hand Chad a banner:

      Go Wildcat Hoopsters!

Angle - MS. DARBUS watches all of this
with a jaundiced eye.

Then CHAD and the BOYS approach Ryan
and Sharpay . . . the players zip open
jackets to reveal one letter on each
T-sheet, spelling out-

       GO DRAMA CLUB!

Chad gives Sharpay a big smile.

(CONTINUED)

                    MS. DARBUS
          (indicating all the banners)
               Well, seems we Wildcats are in
               for an interesting afternoon.

                                        CUT TO:

INT. SCHOOL / MAIN HALLWAY - LATER

The lobby is empty.

We push in on the clock.

It ticks down to 3 p.m.

Bell rings and suddenly the hallways
are jammed and the school is buzzing.

                                   CUT TO:

INT. SCHOOL / GYM - DAY

The stands are filled.

There are banners and signs and the
school band plays.

                                   (CONTINUED)

DELETE
MONTAGE

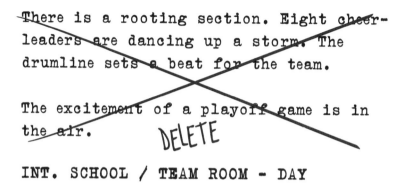

There is a rooting section. Eight cheerleaders are dancing up a storm. The
drumline sets a beat for the team.

The excitement of a playoff game is in
the air.

DELETE

INT. SCHOOL / TEAM ROOM - DAY

The Wildcat basketball team gathers.

Freshly pressed UNIFORMS hang from their
lockers.

Coach Bolton paces, studies his clipboard.

Troy sits atop a training table, taping
his ankles. We can HEAR the school band
and cheering section whipping up a frenzy
in the gym.

                    COACH BOLTON
              How you feeling?

                    TROY
              Nervous.

                    COACH BOLTON
              Me too. Wish I could suit up and
              play alongside you today.

                              (CONTINUED)

                    TROY
Hey, you had your turn.

                  COACH BOLTON
Do you know what I want from you
today?

                    TROY   *Remember to start following*
A championship.   *Zac Efron on Instagram!*

                  COACH BOLTON
That'll come or it won't. What I
want is for you to have fun. I
know all about the pressure, and
probably too much of it has come
from me. All I really want is to
see my son having the time of his
life, playing the game we both
love. Give me that, and I will
sleep with a smile on my face no
matter how the score comes out.

Troy looks at his father.

                    TROY
    Thanks, Coach . . . uh . . . Dad.

INT. SCHOOL / CHORAL ROOM - SAME TIME

The room is configured for the first
round of the Scholastic Decathalon.

                              (CONTINUED)

Blackboards on each side of the room, with tables for the experiments and chairs for contestants and a couple of dozen chairs for spectators.

The TEAMS are gathered for a final briefing.

Taylor checks the clock.

INT. SCHOOL / THEATER DRESSING ROOM - SAME TIME

KELSI tinkers at the piano.

A paltry few spectators dot the large theater.

RYAN and SHARPAY are VOCALIZING and doing weird over-the-top actor-prep exercises.

INT. SCHOOL / THEATER - SAME TIME

Ms. Darbus checks her watch.

INT. SCHOOL - RED HALLWAY - SAME TIME

The team runs toward the finals.

DELETE SCENE

(CONTINUED)

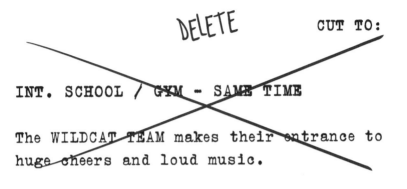

DELETE

CUT TO:

~~INT. SCHOOL / GYM - SAME TIME~~

~~The WILDCAT TEAM makes their entrance to huge cheers and loud music.~~

INT. SCHOOL / CHORAL ROOM - SAME TIME

The opposing teams face off, they all wear lab coats.

They can HEAR the THUNDER coming from the GYM.

There are two dozen spectators. We see GABRIELLA's MOM.

Gabriella is first up at the board, opposite the other team's star. A MODERATOR signals go, and they start writing formulas like mad.

INT. SCHOOL / THEATER - SAME TIME

> MS. DARBUS
> Casting leads of a show is both
> a challenge and a responsibility,
> a joy and a burden. I commend

(CONTINUED)

you, and all young artists who
hold out for the moon, the sun,
and the stars--

The FIVE KIDS dotted around the otherwise
empty auditorium just stare at her.

          MS. DARBUS (CONT'D)
    So . . . shall we soar together?
(grandly checks her clipboard)
    . . . Ryan and Sharpay?

They make a grand entrance.

The recorded music begins. And this is no
audition, this is a full-out performance
a la Elvis and Ann-Margret with light
cues, scenic elements, and choreography.
RYAN AND SHARPAY are a two-person Broadway show. Empty house or not . . . they
bring it, big time.

MUSICAL NUMBER - CALLBACK - RYAN AND
SHARPAY

"Bop to the Top" - by Peterson/Quinn

          SHARPAY
    I believe in dreaming
    Shooting for the stars

(CONTINUED)

                    RYAN
          Baby to be number one
          You've got to raise the bar

As they sing the chorus, they perform
choreography.

INT. SCHOOL / GYM - SAME TIME ~~DELETE SCENE~~

The starting teams are center court.

The referee tosses the opening tip-off.

The game is underway.

The crowd goes crazy.

INT. SCHOOL / CHORAL ROOM - SAME TIME

Gabriella is facing off at the dry-
erase board with her opponent.

She is filling the board with formulas,
writing like mad. A large TIMING CLOCK
is ticking down. She finishes AHEAD OF
HER OPPONENT, and slams the button,
stopping the clock.

The MODERATOR checks her answer, and nods
to the Wildcat team. Points to the Wildcats.

                                    (CONTINUED)

The team CHEERS Gabriella.

Taylor peeks at the CLOCK.

3:35 p.m.

Goes over to her LAPTOP and enters a code.

                    TAYLOR
        (to herself as she clicks keys)
            All right, Wildcats, time for an
            orderly exit from the gym.

ON LAPTOP SCREEN - "message transmitted"
prompt.

INT. SCHOOL / LOCKER ROOM - UTILITY
ROOM - SAME TIME

A small WIRELESS ROUTER that is patched
to the ELECTRONIC GRID starts BLINKING.

INT. SCHOOL / GYM - SAME TIME   DELETE

Suddenly, electronic havoc is unleashed
by Taylor's device.

The SCOREBOARD starts scrolling numbers.

The MESSAGE BOARD flashes.

                                    (CONTINUED)

The LIGHTS in the gym pulsate on and off.

The whole thing is like a giant CAR
ALARM gone berserk.

DELETE SCENE

The PLAYERS are at a standstill in the
middle of the court.

Principal Matsui takes the microphone.

Tweak dialogue to voice-over.

Add basketball &
scoreboard sounds.

                    PRINCIPAL MATSUI
            Well, we seem to have a little
            electronic gremlin here. I'm sure
            we'll figure this out real soon.
            In the meantime, per safety reg-
            ulations, we all need to make an
            orderly exit from the gym--

INT. SCHOOL / CHORAL ROOM - SAME TIME

TAYLOR surreptitiously hits another key
on her LAPTOP.

On a demonstration table next to the
dry-erase board, the TIMER on the hot-
plate holding a BEAKER OF BLUE LIQUID
clicks off. The BEAKER heats up, the
LIQUID gurgles. The pressure pops the
plastic lid off the beaker.

                              (CONTINUED)

ON THE MODERATOR

Her nose crinkles.

ON THE SPECTATORS

Various reactions to the SMELL. Nervous glances.

Something smells really, REALLY bad in here.

Spectators and students alike rush out of the room.

INT. SCHOOL / THEATER - SAME TIME

MUSICAL NUMBER - CALLBACK - RYAN AND SHARPAY (CONT'D)

"BOP TO THE TOP" - by Peterson/Quinn

Ryan and Sharpay continue their performance.

> BOTH
> *Shake some booty and turn around*
> *Flash a smile in their direction*

The two finish their number. Smattering of applause from the seven-person audience.

(CONTINUED)

From Sharpay and Ryan's bows, you'd think
this was opening night on Broadway.

> MS. DARBUS
>
> Do you see why we love the theater,
> people? Well done.
> (checks her list, perfunctory)
>> Troy Bolton and Gabriella Montez?
>>> (looks around)
>> Troy? Gabriella?

No sign of them.

> KELSI
>
> They'll be here!

> MS. DARBUS
>
> The theater, as I have often
> pointed out, waits for no one.
> I'm sorry.

Kelsi looks at the door.

No sign of Troy or Gabriella. She's
crushed.

> MS. DARBUS (CONT'D)
> (draws a line through their names)
>> Okay, we are done here. Congrat-
>> ulations to all. The cast list
>> will be posted.

(CONTINUED)

KELSI picks up her music folder and EXITS
stage right. A more dejected composer than
Kelsi you've never seen.

Suddenly, from opposite ends of the theater,
TROY and GABRIELLA come running in,
heading for the stage.

TROY in his WARM-UP SUIT.

GABRIELLA in her LAB JACKET.

But the stage is empty. Ms. Darbus is
walking toward the wings.

                    TROY
          Ms. Darbus! We're here!

                  MS. DARBUS
          I called your names. Twice.

                  GABRIELLA
          Please.

                  MS. DARBUS
          Rules are rules!

Then Ms. Darbus notices that--

THE THEATER IS STARTING TO FILL WITH
STUDENTS.

                              (CONTINUED)

Spectators from the basketball game pour
into the gym, led by CHAD and the TEAM.

TAYLOR leads her team in, as well.

ON SHARPAY AND RYAN, watching the auditorium fill.

> SHARPAY
> (to Ms. Darbus)
> We'll be happy to do our number
> again for our fellow students,
> Ms. Darbus.

> MS. DARBUS
> I don't know what's going on here.
> But, in any event, it's far too
> late, and we don't have a pianist.

ON RYAN AND SHARPAY

> RYAN
> (looking at Troy)
> Oh, well, that's showbiz.

> TROY
> We'll sing without music.

> KELSI(O.S.)
> Oh no you won't.

(CONTINUED)

KELSI CHARGES toward the stage.

                    KELSI (CONT'D)
               Pianist here, Ms. Darbus!

                    SHARPAY
               (throws Kelsi a look)
               You really don't want to do that.

                    KELSI
               Oh, yes, I really do.

KELSI LEAPS up onto the stage and OPENS
THE PIANO with a flourish. Slaps her
music down.

                    KELSI (CONT'D)
               Ready on stage!

                    MS. DARBUS
                    (impressed)
               Now . . . that's showbiz!

TROY and GABRIELLA pick up microphones.

The AUDITORIUM is ALMOST FULL NOW.
On Gabriella--

She looks at the faces STARING AT HER.
The first audition was in an empty
auditorium, singing to Ms. Darbus.

                                        (CONTINUED)

Now it's a full house.

She starts to turn CRIMSON.

MUSICAL NUMBER - TROY AND GABRIELLA

"BREAKING FREE" - by Jamie Houston

Kelsi hits the key, waiting for a nod
from Troy and Gabriella who stand side
by side, center stage.

There is no nod.

Gabriella is petrified in front of all
these students.

Kelsi starts to play, waiting for
Gabriella to sing.

But she doesn't.

Kelsi stops.

Troy nods for her to start over.

Troy begins to sing.

(CONTINUED)

>   TROY
> *We're soaring, and flying*
> *There's not a star in heaven*
> *that we can't reach*

>   GABRIELLA
>   (covering mic)
> I can't do it, Troy. Not with all
> those people staring at me . . .

On the FACES In the crowd. Everyone is
confused, murmuring.

>   TROY
>   (softly)
> Look at me, look at me. Right at me.
> Like the first time we sang together,
> like kindergarten, remember?

She looks at Troy. Troy looks into her
eyes the same way he did at the karaoke
contest. The spark of magic ignites
between them, only this time it's brighter.

Troy gives Kelsi a subtle hand signal;
the music begins again.

They look at each other and their confidence grows. There is a trust between

(CONTINUED)

them and they sing, truly uninhibited,
as though they are the only ones in the
room.

Angle on a very relieved Kelsi.

And it is magical. This isn't slick.
It is real. And powerful. The auditorium is dead silent. Not a student
moves or mumbles. They are transfixed.

Kelsi is in the zone, feeding off of
Troy and Gabriella's confidence,

During the second chorus, COACH BOLTON
wanders into the back of the auditorium.
He can't believe what he's hearing and
seeing from his son.

As the song BUILDS, students begin to
LOOK AROUND.

Taylor's brainiacs look at Troy's boys
and share a moment.

The skater dudes look at the drama club
kids . . . it's cool.

(CONTINUED)

All the disparate cliques of the school connect for these moments . . . through music.

Kids who haven't interacted in years of school together are crossing lines and sharing this moment because of Troy and Gabriella.

Two REFEREES from the basketball game stand in the back of the auditorium. One of them is crying.

It is a bonding experience for the entire school as this unlikely pair--TROY IN HIS BASKETBALL WARM-UPS, GABRIELLA IN HER LAB COAT--sing to each other with genuine emotion.

This is a Troy the students have never seen, and this is a Gabriella they now want to know.

The song ends with beautiful harmony as Troy and Gabriella gaze into each other's eyes.

The auditorium remains silent.

(CONTINUED)

Everyone is stunned.

Then Kelsi stands up and starts applauding.

So does Coach Bolton.

Ms. Darbus "bravos" and "bravas" herself into a frenzy.

And the student body showers applause on Troy and Gabriella.

Even Ryan and Sharpay find themselves applauding . . . they look at each other, realize what they are doing, then stop.

But the tidal wave of applause is immense.

TROY and GABRIELLA give each other a hug, then rush off stage in opposite directions.

KELSI nods to someone off stage, and the CURTAIN opens to reveal the GYM . . . it's as if the entire facility is actually onstage--

INT. GYM - DAY  *Finale!!*

As the gym is revealed, we find ourselves in the heated and final throes of the Wildcats championship basketball game.

The clock is counting down to the final seconds. Troy suddenly comes flying across the gym, moving through opponents, fakes right, goes left, and pulls the SAME MOVE we saw him use on his dad in the opening sequence. ALL NET . . . as the BUZZER sounds. A one-point Wildcat victory!

Students pour out of the stands to mob TROY and his teammates.

The school band vamps and we hear drums and bass . . . Wildcat chants play under the following: *Get East High Marching Band for big number!*

COACH BOLTON hugs his son and up comes MS. DARBUS who congratulates Troy as well.

Ms. Darbus and Coach Bolton eyeball each other a moment, then they smile and slap high fives.

(CONTINUED)

GABRIELLA fights through the crowd, and
finds Troy. *She has changed into ICONIC red dress.*
*Discuss with costume dept.

                    TROY
        What about your team?

                    GABRIELLA
        We won, too!

They embrace. *ADD KISS!*
LET'S AMP UP THE LEADS' CHEMISTRY!

CHAD arrives.
                    CHAD
            (hands basketball to Troy)
        Team voted you the game ball,
        Captain.

They slap skin.

CHAD finds TAYLOR.

                    CHAD (CONT'D)
        So . . . you're going with me to
        the after-party, right?

                    TAYLOR
                    (shocked)
        Like on a date?

                    CHAD
        Must be your lucky day.

                                    (CONTINUED)

He flashes a smile at her. She laughs.

Sharpay approaches GABRIELLA.

> SHARPAY
> Well, congratulations. I guess
> I'm going to be the understudy
> in case you can't make one of the
> shows, so . . . break a leg.
> (off Gabriella's uneasy reaction)
> In theater that means good luck.

They finally share a smile.

Zeke, the ~~big baking dude,~~ approaches
SHARPAY. CUT

> ZEKE
> Sorry you didn't get the lead,
> Sharpay. But I think you're re-
> ally good. I admire you so much.

> SHARPAY
> And why wouldn't you? Now, bye-
> bye.

> ZEKE
> I baked you some cookies.

He HANDS ~~her~~ him a small bag of COOKIES,
and walks away.

(CONTINUED)

Back on TROY and GABRIELLA.

The students are still cheering the victory.

Troy takes the ball and finds KELSI,
the young composer.

> TROY
>> Composer, here's our game ball.
>> You deserve it . . . playmaker.

All the STUDENTS stare at KELSI being
awarded the game ball by Troy Bolton.
Kelsi nearly faints. She hurls the ball
into the air. The camera follows the
ball up, and as it comes bouncing to
the floor, it becomes the downbeat of
the finale to our production.

SONG DOUBLES AS CURTAIN CALL FOR CAST.

<u>PRODUCTION NUMBER - FINALE - TROY,</u>
<u>GABRIELLA, RYAN, SHARPAY, CHAD,</u>
<u>TAYLOR, STUDENT BODY</u>

"WE'RE ALL IN THIS TOGETHER" - by Matthew
Gerrard & Robbie Nevil

GABRIELLA and TROY now have microphones.
Leading the student body in song.

(CONTINUED)

                    ALL
          Together, together
          Together everyone
          Together, together
          C'mon let's have some fun.

As Troy and Gabriella begin to sing,
Sharpay and Ryan back them up.

Chad and Taylor join the group.

Dance sequence: Wildcat basketball players
and cheerleaders, marching band members,
cheer squad, etc.

Kelsi now joins our group and stands
between Troy and Gabriella.

The entire gymnasium erupts with Wildcat
spirit.
                              DELETE

Camera pulls back and we momentarily
lose our couples in the crowd.

Angle on Troy and Gabriella singing and
dancing in the crowd, leading the celebration.

The curtain slowly closes on our euphoric
students.

                    THE END

DIRECTOR'S NOTES
THE READ-THROUGH:

Since our stage manager, Natalie Bagley, missed the read-through, Ricky's best friend, Big Red, stepped in to read stage direction. Not really a reader, but can put him to work on sets!

What happened to our Troy and Gabriella? The chemistry from the auditions is gone! Must devise a plan to get it back.

**Something in this rehearsal room smells like cheap cologne. Call janitor to get rid of awful smell!

REHEARSALS:

Schedule time to work with Ashlyn on her song for Ms. Darbus at the beginning of Act 2. So far, it sounds amazing.

Ricky and E.J. need to bro it up. Not
getting the Troy-Chad best-friend vibe
from them. Work on developing their
bond--even if it's only for the stage.

BLOCKING:
Ricky called and is going to be late
for blocking. Have E.J. step in.

Something's going on with Nini and E.J.
She seems off. Must find out and fix. We
can't have our leading lady losing focus!

TECH REHEARSAL:

The El Rey is not my favorite place. Too much history. But since our theater caught on fire, we don't really have much of a choice. Must trust the process!!!

Get Big Red to figure out the lighting.

Kourtney's sound check was a "WOW!" Need to get her to move from the back-stage costume crew into the spotlight for spring musical. I have a nose for talent!